ONE BILLION FACES

(Short Stories)

Mario Barbatti

This is a work of fiction. All characters and events portrayed in this book are either fictitious or used fictitiously.

www.barbatti.org/one-billion-faces
One Billion Faces (Short Stories) / Mario Barbatti

ISBN 978-2-9569724-1-9 (kindle)
ISBN 978-2-9569724-2-6 (pdf)
ISBN 978-2-9569724-3-3 (mobi)
ISBN 978-2-9569724-4-0 (epub)
ISBN 978-2-9569724-5-7 (paperback)

First Edition
Cover photo by Ryan Holloway on Unsplash.

To Marie.
She will never read this book.
She will never know how important she was to help me
finish it.

Table of Contents

THE GHOSTS

I. The Empty House

"You should be kidding me!" shouted Brannon when he found the corridor's lights off once more.

The house was empty. All his mates left for the weekend. He stayed. It wouldn't be too much fun to travel with the uncomfortable plaster entirely immobilizing his broken leg.

Standing by the bathroom's door, he groped for the switch and turned the lights on. Brannon browsed the long, deserted corridor giving access to the sleeping rooms. At the other end, he could see part of the vast space of the living room. Everything was silent, as it should be.

Brannon never told anyone, but he wasn't totally comfortable in the dark. It wasn't like some childish fear, but rather an instinctive, unease feeling from the nothingness surrounding him.

Goofily dragging the plaster, he walked back to his room. Near his door, the lights went off again. But this time, he could swear he heard something coming from the living room. Up to then, he thought that the lights were annoyingly switching on and off for the whole day due to some electrical glitch; he was planning to call the landlord first thing on Monday. But now, he wasn't sure he was really alone at home anymore. Maybe someone stayed behind?

Brannon turned the lights on at the nearest switch and inspected each door. At the far back, the shared bathroom from where he came. Next, Carl's and Mike's doors, one at each side of the corridor. Both closed. Then, his own door where he was standing by. Just across, Tricia's one. Both also closed. Then, …wait, then? Between his door and the open space of the living room, there was still another door. How did he never notice it? Was that another guest room? The wall around it was too wide for a storage room. Was there any guest living there?

Brannon hobbled as fast as he could to check it. The door was slightly open. He knocked and called, "Hi, anyone in there?" No answer.

He gently pushed the door and glanced at the inside. The room was dark, but the streetlight coming through the window revealed it was, in fact, another standard guest room. The bed, the desk arranged just like in his own room.

How did he never see that before? He was utterly puzzled. The room was empty, but there was a laptop on the desk and a few pieces of cloths hanging on the chair; a new guest, for sure.

He was already leaving, closing the door when someone behind him just said, "Hi!"

* * *

Brannon was still recovering his breath, when the person, a girl, coming from the living room approached. "Sorry, I didn't mean to startle you." Despite the apology, her smile showed she was having fun with the situation, while Brannon was fighting to avoid blushing at his ridiculous overreaction. "I'm Sarah. I don't think we've been introduced," she continued.

"Hi, Brannon. Sorry, I didn't …" he wasn't sure about what to say.

Sarah just interrupted to ease him, "That's fine."

Brannon continued, "I thought everyone had left for the weekend. I wasn't expecting anyone at home. Even less a new guest. To be sincere," he wasn't sure whether he should mention that, "I was also surprised by your room. I've never noticed it."

"What do you mean by 'new guest'?" asked Sarah, intrigued. "I've been living here since early spring."

"Are you teasing me?" Brannon asked, annoyed. "I've been living here since September too. We'd certainly have met before, then."

Sarah wasn't smiling anymore, and Brannon felt she was serious. He tried to play it cool, "I'm sure there is a reasonable explanation. Most likely we're on some mismatching schedule."

Sarah nodded uncertainly.

"Well, I'm enrolled at the Languages college. You?" continued Brannon.

It took Sarah a while to answer; she was still lost in her wonders. "I, I'm at the Tech college; engineering," she finally replied.

"Look," she continued, "I'm not sure about what's happening here. To find someone I never saw in the house, peeking at my room, and telling me that has been my room's neighbor for months… It's a little too much to take in."

Brannon agreed. His guts were filled with unease, the same as he felt in the dark. He tried to lightly reason, "Take from my viewpoint: I'm alone at home, and the lights keep flicking on and off. Then, a blond girl appears out of nowhere to tell me she lives in a room next to mine; a room I'm sure I never saw before." His attempt at humor sounded fake and nervous.

Sarah decided to ease the mood with a pun, "Maybe you're a ghost."

"Impossible!" played Brannon along, "Have you ever seen a black ghost?"

She giggled, "Fine; maybe we're both ghosts."

"Easy to check, miss," said Brannon extending his hand for a handshake.

Sarah approached; as their hands touched, their faces twisted in a mix of shock and curiosity when they noticed that they slightly interpenetrated. Not entirely, but their skins just didn't lie where they were supposed to. Their handshake looked just like a poorly photoshopped picture. The touch feeling, however, was regular. Brannon felt Sarah's skin soft and nicely cold; she felt his grip firm and warm.

They didn't give up to fear. They rested holding hands amazed by the eerie experience.

Sarah, still staring at their hands, was the first to say something: "Definitely, one of us is a ghost."

"Or both of us," amended Brannon, also frozen at sight.

* * *

Brannon and Sarah took seats on the sofas in the living room. Both had been silent. They didn't know what to say.

"I think, therefore I am, right?" rhetorically asked Brannon. Sarah didn't reply. Brannon reached out for a mug on the center table. He touched it gently. He was comforted by the natural feeling of the ceramics, cold and smooth; his finger followed the embossments of the college's logo imprinted on the surface. But the relief vanished at the bad photoshop effect once more: the contours of his hand and the mug overlapped bizarrely.

Sarah followed Brannon's experiment herself and touched a book resting on the table. Just like Brannon, she could perfectly feel it. And, again like him, her hand slightly penetrated the object. An expression of horror came to her face when she failed to grab the book. Her hand just slipped through it, as if the book were glued to the surface.

Sarah's failed attempt at grabbing the book scared them both more than any of the crazy experiences they have had so far. Brannon tried to push and lift several objects in the room. At each failure, he felt his guts revolving and his heart pounding—should a ghost have heartbeats?

"What are we? Death souls haunting a house?" Brannon asked while nervously laughing at the absurd of that description.

Sarah was trying to be objective when she asked, "Who does live here?"

"What?"

"Just answer me, please. Who does live in this house?" repeated her.

Brannon guessed Sarah's intention and decided to play along, "Well, besides me—and apparently you—Mike, Tricia, and Carl."

"Where were you born?", "When is your birthday?", "What did you have for breakfast today?" she asked these and several other personal questions. Although Brannon answered each of them, his recollections of facts, places, and people were odd. His memories felt fake to himself, like a lousy excuse for a lost appointment.

"How did you break your leg?"

Brannon remembered the ski accident a couple of weeks before. He could recall the sharp, intense pain. At the same time, he felt as if it were the first time he ever heard of that accident.

The impotence facing his own mind playing games turned Brannon angry. He was furious. "Stop with this shit!" he shouted, as to stop the fake memories to flood his brain. "Isn't it enough to be a ghost, but I must be trapped in a house with a fucking over-rational, annoying…" He didn't finish the sentence. The word "trapped" rang like a loud alarm for both. They simultaneously looked at the exit door. Sarah ran towards it and cursed when the knob didn't answer to her grip, just like any other object she touched.

Brannon tried to smash a window with his bare hands. The glass stood still. He cried for help, even though the street outside was utterly empty. He shouted and cursed loudly, irrationally diving into his anger and frustration. His body looked enormous and disproportional to the environment around. Lights went on and off at his bursts of rage. The TV set turned on, few light bulbs burned.

In this meanwhile, Sarah was sitting on the floor, bracing herself and resting against the exit door she failed to open. She cried compulsively, incapable of controlling her emotions and remaining rational as she wished.

Suddenly, an electric buzz filled the living room. Both halted immediately in silence. Sarah joined Brannon at the window. The world outside the house seemed to have been reduced to a small patch of snowed lawn, surrounded by a sphere of impenetrable darkness. The dark sphere was slowly closing on them, swallowing everything on the way.

Sarah and Brannon held hands, as well as they could do under their condition. The darkness invaded the house, through the ceiling, the corridor, the walls. There was nowhere to run.

Their last words before they were swallowed into the nothingness came from Sarah: "Do ghosts die?"

II. The broken House

"Unfortunately, there's no way around. I'll have to reboot the whole AI system." Peter was about to start the shutting-down procedure from his tablet.

Clara, sitting on a sofa in the large living room, tried to slow him down a bit. "Are you sure? If you do shut the system down, we'll lose months of grown personality. I'm really fond of Brannon. He's not only great managing the house. He's, you know, kind of part of the family by now."

"I'm sorry, Clara. I can't do anything else at this point. The system diagnostic shows that the AI started to develop a double-personality dysfunction. The situation is irreversible. From now on, it will just degrade. The AI personalities are conflicting, giving contradictory commands. This is the reason for all these devices flicking like in a haunted house. If we don't reboot it now, things will get worse."

Clara looked around at the appliances, randomly switching on and off. "Yes, I understand," she said. "It's… I just feel like euthanizing a friend."

"You know Brannon is just an algorithmic expression for our comfort. *It* isn't alive and doesn't feel anything," explained Peter, stressing the pronoun.

"Of course, I do know that," answered Clara, annoyed by Peter's patronizing tone. "I just can't avoid developing some feeling for him, *for it*, whatever."

"I reboot the system now, and we'll have a fully grown, healthy personality within a couple of weeks," stated Peter. "I'll surely miss Brannon, too. But we'll get used to the new AI."

"Right," agreed Clara. "Just make sure we won't have to put another friend down within a few months."

"Fine," asserted Peter pressing the restart command.

FUTURE CANVAS

It's a staggering view. Every time I have the opportunity to visit the observatory above the solar panels, I can't stop admiring the Dyson cap surrounding me for a hundred million kilometers in every direction. The golden-brown ocean of an infinite number of moving crafts shining under the Sun takes my breath away. I used to travel here often when I was a student, especially if I was trying to impress a date. Now, as an assistant researcher, I spend most of my time in my office, working on simulations of the caps' history. My visits to the observatory are getting rarer.

Either due to my métier—I'm an expert on physical-history with an emphasis on population evolution—or the mesmerizing feeling they fill me, I'm always wondering about the astonishing numbers concerning absolutely any aspect of humanity. We just completed sixteen thousand Earth years of civilization since the agricultural revolution, four thousand years since the industrial revolution, and we count one hundred thousand trillion alive souls today. The question that fills each minute of my day, and I bring to bed every evening is what's our limit.

Every time we thought we reached our maximum boundaries, we discovered we were wrong. At the industrial revolution, we thought food resources wouldn't allow surpassing the meager first billion humans; but then massive advances in agricultural techniques postponed the proclaimed apocalypse. Two hundred years passed, we declared that the end was near once more; that Earth resources wouldn't be enough to sustain over ten billion people. The shift to renewable energies and synthetic food proved us wrong once more. Few hundred years later, we believed that the limit was finally reached when one hundred billion people wouldn't fit on the old planet. But then, the first orbital cities started to grow, tapping at an incredible potential.

Suddenly, we figured out we could overcome our primeval instincts like that we must have a floor under our feet or that food must ultimately grow from the soil. When we got rid of these restraining myths, we found the freedom to spread throughout the whole solar system. Orbital cities grew around every planet, every major moon, which essentially became our suppliers of raw material for all life in space. Even mother Earth used to barely be a commodities supplier, inhabited by only a few billion people dedicated to exporting minerals, air, and water to the orbital cities.

Common to all those outdated apocalyptic prophecies was the misunderstanding of the stout feedback loop between technology, economy, and population. All Malthusian thinkers understood well how new technological advancements led to productivity improvements, which in turn triggered population growth. The point they usually missed is that population growth was a significant trigger of new technological advancements, by economically enabling them. Thus, when the industrial revolution four thousand years ago led us to overcome the one billion people mark and raised the worries about food supply, it was precisely the high demand for food from those one billion people that made economically viable to implement technology-intense agriculture.

Then, we needed two billion people to make nuclear fission energy viable; seven billion people to make solar energy sustainable; ten billion people to replace the whole energy grid for renewable sources; one hundred billion, to make portable nuclear fusion viable. Now, with one hundred thousand trillion people, we are reaching a new limit for sustainable population size that our current technological development with an energy grid based on solar power and fusion allows.

The Dyson caps are two semi-spherical shells, three hundred million kilometers across, covering the poles of the solar system, having the Sun as their center. I live in the north cap, about forty five degrees above the solar system orbital plane. The other cap is alike but in the south.

The name cap may invoke a solid shell, but nothing is farther from the truth. The cap is formed by tens of trillions of independent crafts. Some autonomous, some inhabited. Some crafts are tinny and aimed for a few dozen people, others are gigantic hyper-metropolis where hundreds of millions people live. The crafts have the most diverse shapes and designs. But they usually share two features in common, a fusion-propelled engine and a set of solar energy collectors.

My city, for instance, is pretty standard in this sector. It's a cylindric craft with about one-kilometer radius and half-kilometer long, where 2.5 million people live in one hundred concentric stores. The craft rotates with a four-minutes period, which grants a comfortable $0.13g$ gravity in the outer stores, about the same as in the Moon. The city owns about sixty thousand square meters of solar collectors made of thin sheets of photovoltaic and photosynthetic materials. They move independently of the craft, keeping always oriented towards the Sun. We still have a forty percent energetic deficit, which must be supplemented by energy imports from other cities.

The crafts don't necessarily move synchronized with each other, neither even at the same speed. They try to optimize their exposure to the Sun before they hide in the shadow of another craft. For this reason, rather than resembles a solid layer, each cap looks like a living body, with its uncountable parts emerging and submerging in an infinite ocean.

Every three hundred cycles of twenty-four hours, my city resurfaces in its most internal position in the cap—the "summer solstice," before starting its circular motion back towards the outer layers. One hundred fifty days later, it reaches the outmost cap layer during the "winter solstice."

The caps were never an engineering project on their own. They evolved naturally in the last two thousand years. As the orbital cities grew, they spread throughout the inner solar orbits as close as that of Venus. At first, this wasn't a problem. Space is vast; space is an infinite commodity, one thought. That was apparently true until the population reached a thousand trillion people. We then felt the first signs of the overpopulation. The number of crafts carrying extra-orbital cities exploded, and they started to compete for a better spot of solar irradiation.

Those were dark ages resting for almost one thousand years; a period sadly known as the Shadow wars.

History may be told from the human perspective. The rise and the fall of the nations; their economic and political structures; their achievements and their battles; their rulers and their people. Nevertheless, when it comes to the caps, their history is better told by physics; more precisely, physical-history, my specialty.

In the last two millennia, trillions of crafts self-organized in the form of the two semi-spherical caps, induced by different restraints. They should maximize their exposure to the Sun but without coming into too close orbits, where heat and ionizing radiation start to be a significant problem; they must avoid collision, shadow, and scaping jets from the other crafts; they should avoid lying on the solar system orbital plan, where they could be retaliated by planetary colonies and orbital-cities; finally, they must keep an accelerated motion to grant some gravity. Taking these restraints together, any simulation model (like those I develop for a living) shows that the formation of the polar Dyson caps was the natural outcome, independent of any global projects, peace conventions, trade agreements, economic needs, and all these things we humans think of having any control on.

Ah, but the view… I left the city for some holidays at the observatory. Here, ten thousand kilometers above the inner cap surface, I can admire the caps in all their glory. The "sky" is mostly dark, but not entirely black as in empty space. Covered by the south cap as far as sixteen light-minutes from here, the sky is more like a deep dark brown. It's midday, and the Sun shines straight above me. Venus and Mercury shine just below the Sun. Besides that, there is a handful of feeble bright spots. They aren't stars, but the lights from the biggest hyper-metropolis in the nearest sectors of the south cap, at about two light-minutes from here. The fact I can see them with naked eyes attests the overwhelming dimensions of these cities, each one with over one hundred trillion inhabitants. No other feature can be distinguished there in the south cap, of course.

The sky is crossed by a deep black ribbon, cutting a 360° diagonal in the dark brown, separating the north and south caps. It marks the solar system orbital plane. The ribbon is not only set to allow the sunlight to get to the planets and their orbital cities. Another main reason is that without this opening, the caps would turn into a deadly oven of trapped radiation. Through and beyond the black ribbon, I can see Earth, Mars, the outer giants, and the stars. Earth, although it is the nearest planet, is just a pale rocky spot, far from the romantic blue marble it iconically was in the far past.

The sky is still full of crafts above and below us, but they are not integrated into the cap. They are metallurgic plants, food processing units, and other large industries, which either own a special status (like the observatory itself) or pay for continuous exposition to the Sun. There is a frenetic movement of cargo and passenger crafts boarding and leaving them.

Ten thousand kilometers below me, the myriad of moving panels of the north cap washes out into a flat "landscape," extending in every direction to infinity. The reflex of the Sun on the solar collectors and their frames draws the golden-brown landscape. There is no horizon; there is no feeling of curvature, of course. The flatland smoothly fades into the sky, as if immense dark walls surrounding us sprouted from the floor. Replacing the stars, the biggest metropolitan centers in this sector of the north are bright spots shining in the cap.

One of the things I love the most about this view from the observatory is that the cap below looks so peaceful. At this distance, the crafts constantly emerging and submerging don't feel chaotic. From here, all this movement is harmonious. The cap looks like an infinite breathing living tissue, dancing at silent music.

Everything about humans is superlative. Every aspect—languages, currencies, cultures, religions, nations—is counted in trillions. We could say we live in the golden age of anthropology: just chose your combination of cultural markers, and you will find it somewhere in the caps.

There is nothing like a central government. There are protocols, which are generally followed. (For instance, how to proceed if a craft's engine fails. To let it by itself could lead to a chain reaction of collisions, as in fact it, unfortunately, happens occasionally.) The largest empires in history are in the cap. And they are counted in thousands! In the caps, we will find as many cruel dictatorships as liberal bureaucracies. There are luxurious cities where the wealthiest enjoy lifespans of hundreds of years and gargantuan slams where thousands of trillions fight day-by-day to ensure the recycled air.

Our ancestors on Earth had no idea how easy their lives were. They were naturally endowed with air, water, heat, photosynthesis, gravity, and radiation protection. In space, we must secure each of them through unstoppable work. In a middle-class city like where I live, all these commodities are delivered at satisfactory levels, with access to the essential probiotics without which our bodies would turn into an atrophied mush. But most of the people still live in cities without proper infrastructure. Freezing hell-holes in the outer shells of the caps, where they have no option but breathing carbonated air.

Human history has always been about overcoming constraints. With the agricultural revolution sixteen thousand years ago, we learned how to optimize food supplies by controlled storage of chemical energy in plants and animals. That gave us a carrying capacity of a few hundred million people restricted to Earth. Then, in the wake of the industrial revolution four thousand years ago, we learned how to optimize the production and transport of goods and information, enabling diverse sources of energy, especially fossil. Our carrying capacity suddenly raised to ten billion people also pined to Earth. Next, the gravitational revolution a few centuries later, based on space elevators, released us from the Earth surface constraint by the first time. It enabled billions of people to populate the pre-cap orbital cities. However, we remained dependent on commodities produced on Earth, especially organic substances. Finally, a new industrial revolution released us from all those constraints. We mastered the up-scaling synthesis of complex organic matter directly from trivial substances like carbon dioxide and hydrogen chloride, which can be found everywhere in the solar system. By the first time ever, we didn't need to grow food, polymers, and all sort of organic goods from animals and plants. By the first time, humans as species didn't need to remain close to Earth or any planetary body. (I've heard of political groups proposing to go back to the origins and harvesting plants to complement our nutritional needs. For me, however, the idea of feeding on other living beings is awfully disgusting.)

But we still have constraints, and they are related to energy consumption. Currently, we need about one hundred million square kilometers of solar collectors per one billion people. Giving the surface of the caps, this energy consumption level sets a carrying capacity for the human population at about one hundred thousand trillion people, just about the current number of inhabitants of the solar system. The new Malthusians are back; they are everywhere proclaiming that the end is near.

I'm sitting at the observatory. Saturn shines in the black ribbon. There is some breathtaking thing just happening there. It will once more prove the Malthusians wrong.

Some ancient philosophers used to think that humans had no special role in biological evolution. That our species was just another one among uncountable species. But this understanding was an illusion of those thinkers trapped on the blue planet. Today, we are the only macroscopic organism in the whole solar system, and it is clear that there was something exceptional about our species. It is as if the dramatic diversity of multicellular life forms spawned during one billion years on Earth was only a test field for natural evolution to select its champion, us.

The development of the Dyson caps required an enormous amount of matter. For the last two thousand years, we mined Earth for its invaluable water, gases, biomes, and minerals to the point that only a dry and dark volcanic dead planet surrounded by a thin atmospheric layer is left. It wasn't the proudest chapter of our history when we forced billions to either emigrate from the planet into the orbital cities or starve on the collapsing environment. But which other options did we have to sustain the growing population?

We've harvested Venus and Mars atmospheres for their carbon dioxide (which is the basis of our nutrients through the artificial photosynthesis, and ultimately of our bodies), we intensively import hydrogen from Jupiter to fuel our engines. The Moon, Deimos and Phobos, Ceres, Vesta, Pallas, and Hygiea, Io, Europa, Ganymede, and Callisto: is there any large rock from here to Jupiter we don't have at least one large mining plant?

I look down at the cap. If I focus at distant points, where I can't distinguish individual crafts anymore, it resembles a continuous waving dark-golden fabric, pretty much like the oceans on the ancient Earth, I guess. It feels so distinct from the apparent chaos from within the cap, where the rotating, giant crafts constantly move relative to each other, folding and unfolding their solar panels;

surrounded by uncountable cargo ships and shuttles transporting people in their errands between cities; embedded in a constellation of warning, signaling, and commercial lights.

Many thinkers have compared humans to a virus, some solar system epidemics leaving a trail of dead sidereal bodies behind. Hyperbolic but compelling metaphor. And we may be starting to spread beyond our patient zero. Colonists already left the solar system a few centuries ago towards different destinations nearby. The colony in Proxima Centauri seems to be exceptionally wealthy.

We are at the limit of our energetic capacity. But the stress it causes also forces us to seek opportunities. Nova Beijing, one of the largest and richest hyper-metropolis in the north cap has been importing light from Proxima Centauri! The colony has been sending high-power laser beams to a city's photosynthesis plant in the outskirts of the solar system. It has been an extraordinary engineering effort to place the many relays to refocus the beam all the way through the four light-years between us. A low-power back beam delivers the payment in the form of information, transmitting from scientific data to entertainment products to Proxima Centauri. But as awesome as this interstellar business sounds, harvesting neighbor stars won't solve our short-term energetic deficit. The Saturn solution looks much more promising.

A consortium of some of the most powerful corporations in both caps has been developing a game-changing project. Two decades ago, they started to build the basis to create a black hole orbiting Saturn. When ready and in full activity, its accretion disk pumping Saturn's atmosphere will be a new high-energy source in the solar system, which will be harvested to feed two new small Dyson caps that will be assembled in a high orbit around the planet. The blackhole's orbit should be stable for the next fifty thousand years, after which the black hole will finally fall on Saturn and ultimately eat it from the inside.

The project is monstrous, involving engineering, economical, diplomatic, political, and military plans much beyond anything humans have done on purpose so far. (The kind of enterprise that becomes feasible only one has one hundred thousand trillion people around.) In the last ten years, thousands of giant synchrotrons, each with the diameter of a small moon, have been assembled in a low Saturn's orbit below the rings. The machines were entangled in each other's, looking like a gigantic spaghetti spherical shell. All of them have had their particle beams directed at the same focal point. The theory says that the simultaneous compression of matter into the tiny space must break the strong force barrier, giving birth to a microscopic stable black hole.

This visit to the observatory is special to me. The news is that the black hole creation was a success; and that it is already stable and orbiting Saturn. Through the telescope, the synchrotrons are not visible anymore, as they were, as expected, destroyed by the blast following the black hole emergence. It will also take a century or so until the accretion disc becomes visible and useful. If the project is successful, it will undoubtedly be extended to Uranus and Neptune.

Maybe we're in fact a virus, spreading through the whole solar system, leaving a trail of dead planets on the way. We already started to infect other solar systems. It may be just a matter of time to have every star, every gaseous planet, every black hole in the Milky Way eclipsed by Dyson caps. Sure enough, in this expansion, eventually we will meet some alien civilization. But I wouldn't worry. At this point, I'm sure we're at the top of the galactic food chain, so to say. We're the Spaniards in this intragalactic journey, not the native Americans.

Nevertheless, speaking of "we" as a species in this distant future context is likely inappropriate. Speciation is bound to happen, if it already didn't start in the most isolated regions of the caps. A new biology—a galactic biology—is going to emerge with uncountable new humanoid species diverging from their homo sapiens common ancestor.

It will come the day even the Milk Way will be small for humans and their descendants. I don't doubt that in this distant future, Malthusians will still be there proclaiming the imminent end of the times. However, in this scenario, we will be talking of 10^{28} individuals. Think of the wonders an economic system entangling such population won't be able to accomplish. To jump across the couple of million light-years to start over in Andromeda may well be one of them.

As far as we know now, human spreading will be finally contained only after we colonize every single galaxy in the Local Group. The Maffei group may be, in principle, unreachable due to the universe expansion. But at this point, who would bet it's truly safe from us?

THE BIBELOTS ON THE SHELF

(Flash Stories)

One Billion Faces

I won't bother you on how I got portraits of one billion faces. I will just invite you to come over to watch the first exhibition of my newest creation.

I will only explain that I collected one billion photos of one billion different human faces. One billion adult faces from all over the world, from every country, from every race, every skin color and hair type, every faith and profession.

One billion photos taken from a standard front position, neutral expression, on a plain white background.

I will tell that I created an algorithm to sort all my one billion faces according to their degree of similarity and that, then, I made a movie containing all of them in sequence. You will be shocked when you learn that at 48 frames per second, the film will continuously play for 241 days—eight months—and that, in fact, it has already been playing for weeks now.

You will come over to watch it. You will look at the screen and, for a moment, you will think that it is just a single person staring at the camera. But then you will note that the face is slowly transforming into other faces, always surrounded by a diffuse cloud coming from the merging of different hair types and styles and holding a somewhat undefined color and texture.

Only at that point, you will realize the implications of those one billion sorted faces playing continuously: human faces aren't individual, they form a continuum spectrum with hundreds of people completely unknown to each other, without any family links, but sharing the same face.

I will explain that at the beginning of the movie, things weren't so smooth. There lie the monsters: deformed faces that were on themselves unique. But flicking at 48 fps, I couldn't really see them. It was just the feeling that something was wrong, dreadfully wrong. Then, the ghostly flicking started to converge into a human face smoothly evolving.

You will sit there with me and, for days, you will watch distracted the movie. We will laugh for a few minutes when a funny sequence of baby-like faces spots. But we will be bored when they are still there after hours.

I will tell you how humans are great at recognizing and distinguishing faces. We see faces even where they don't exist. But our brains were shaped to distinguish between individuals within communities of a few thousand people, not one billion.

You will be mild interested when I mention that during the eight months that this movie will continuously play, five million of those faces will die; but that this loss would be more than compensated by the eighty million new faces that will have been born in the same period.

After a couple of weeks, we will be silent. But not due to the hypnotic monotony of the movie. This will be a tense silence. In the beginning, we won't be able to pinpoint what was wrong, but then it will be apparent that the face on the screen is becoming more and more like yours.

After a few minutes, we will be just staring at you at the screen. For twenty seconds, your face will be there. About one thousand faces just like yours. Identical non-genetic twins, who would have remained unknown for you were not for my movie.

You will say that it's no big deal, that you don't feel your individuality threatened by knowing that you shared your face with many other people. But it won't take you long to stand up, tell me that you are tired of this useless movie, and live.

I will stay. I will also see my own face after a few days. I will lie to myself reassuring my self-confidence, too; and I will force myself to persist to the end.

I will sit there, watching the movie for the remaining weeks, until the ghostly monsters at the other extreme of my one billion sorted faces start to flick and the film finishes.

I will remain in the dark room for a long while, wondering whether our feelings and pains, our desires and dreams, our emotions and memories wouldn't also be diluted within a continuum spectrum of one billion souls.

To Live is Too Dangerous

"I tell you, Sir, from all I lived: the most difficult deed isn't a good being and an honest behaving. Really difficult is a defined knowing on what one wants; and having the power to go till the tail of the word." The Devil to Pay in the Backlands, Guimarães Rosa.

For someone who spends his days in front of computer screens, his body is comically covered by scars. He could easily be mistaken for an unlucky war veteran or a goofy criminal. But each of those scars over his forty years of life had the banalest and stupidest reason for being.

His left arm is crossed by two thick and long patches of bright pink skin looking like a skull smile. He got those when he was very young. Apparently, his parents thought that it would be a good idea to let a seven-year-old child go wandering on the street, holding a big glass bottle. Well, it wasn't.

His forehead also brings a scar from that distant past. Distracted playing hide-and-seek, he didn't see the window stool running against him.

He thinks that it wasn't much later when another scar was imprinted on him—that time on his right knee. He was trying to trespass a barbed-wired fence to pick up mangoes from a tree.

From many years later, a tinny cut hides between his fingers in his left hand; a minor kitchen-knife accident. More impressive, however, is the cicatrix on his right wrist. No, it doesn't shamefully denounce a failed suicide attempt, but just a silly slide on a wet bathroom floor.

If you see the big mark cutting through his left elbow, then you would bet that it was to remove a bullet dangerously lodged near his heart. What else could it be? Well, it was, in fact, nothing more than a simple atheroma surgery butchery-performed by an old Hungarian doctor.

And these are only the external marks.

For almost three decades gastritis haunts him, probably engraving scary marks on the inner walls of his stomach, where—he hopes—he will never glance at.

That's not to speak of all those unavoidable emotional scars, whose marks carved in the soul, he doesn't dare to face.

He agrees with Guimarães Rosa's character: to be good and honest isn't even difficult. The difficult task has been to know what he really wants and how he can make it real. Especially with all the scars-to-be hidden ahead in his future, just running invisibly against him, to strike when he least expects… To live is too dangerous, isn't it?

But cautious, he already left instructions for his eventual funeral: he wants to be burned. His ashes must be stored in a jar, in such a way that whenever anyone opens it, he will suddenly burst into a ghostly cloud and grant the person three treasured wishes. This will be his most significant, or, more probably, only legacy.

When Icarus Flew Over the Hidden Side of the Moon

Look at me, Dad, I reached farther than you ever believed.

Now, I feel the wings starting melting. They burn my skin, but it is all worthy.

I fly here above anyone ever flew. I see the moon floating below me. All that remains is the sun and the pure blue sky.

I look down, and I see you there, flying low, flying safely. Are you proud of me, Dad?

I feel the wings melting, and I am afraid.

Is it worth flying here? Who will ever know, who would even care, that an Icarus son of Daedalus once touched the sun and died for that?

Now that I know you can't hear me, I can tell you how much I doubt myself. Sometimes I think that all men in the Agora laughed at me behind my back; that all of them saw me for the fraud I am. Of course, this feeling hurts deep in my soul, but my biggest fear has always been that you ashamedly agreed with them.

This is why I fly here over the hidden side of the moon.

I speak out now that you can't hear me, but have you ever listened to me anyway?

I think you always saw me as a ghost of your expectations. You never saw me for what I am. But only as a second chance for yourself to achieve all that you couldn't accomplish in your own years; to escape this labyrinth that you built and made yourself a prisoner.

I don't blame you, Dad. If anyone is to blame, it's me who was too weak to impose myself. My weakness brought me here where my wings are destined to melt.

I look down, and I see you, so small, so distant from me. My heart squeezes. How ironic is it that I came to touch the sun, but l could never touch you?

I tell you now something I never told anyone. When l was a child, I prayed to the Gods for that I died before you. I couldn't stand the idea that one day you wouldn't be there for me. You looked then so big, so close.

Now that my wingless body freely falls, I realize that I have never really overcome this childish fear. That all my life was a farce waiting for this end, where I give up everything for that you could be proud of me.

I never wanted to fly here, Dad. I don't deserve to fly here. I do fly here only for the right of being here.

Was it worth it?

The Time of My Selfish Altruism

This week, while tinkering with some old stuff that came in my moving from Germany to France, I invented a time-travel device.

It's a different model from those available in the market. Well, as usual, my device allows me to go back in time, always to a parallel timeline. I can also interfere and change that timeline, which is also no surprise: the air displaced by my body volume is already enough to trigger a new sequence of events; you know, just ordinary butterfly effect.

However, what's peculiar about my new time-travel device is that after two minutes visiting some alternative timeline, I'm automatically kicked back to my original timeline.

This is a bit disappointing, I must confess. In two minutes, I can't properly do any of the top-three most-popular time-travel programs: watch dinosaurs, help King Arthur, and kiss Sophia Loren.

I could still go back and do some considerable good for humanity (in the other timeline, naturally), like killing the mother of the guy who invented burger buns before he was born. Those disgusting, stodgy, soft brioches disgrace an otherwise perfectly fine dish. But I'd have to study history to figure out who did it; I'm too lazy to do that. Also, all this terminator plot is too much of a cliché for my taste.

Then, among those forty-eight boxes currently packing my life in a dark French cellar, I kept asking myself: what can I do within two minutes, while visiting any moment of history in a parallel timeline?

I finally figured it out. I decided that I'll dedicate myself to charity. Personal charity, I'd say. In each time travel, I'll help myself on the other timeline. (I modestly call it *mariophilanthropy*.) My goal is to make the multiverse a better place for thousands of Mario Barbattis in need.

The possibilities are literally infinite: starting from the trivial, I could gift my last-week self the Lotto's results; I could deliver a six-pack of cold Leffe to myself in Mülheim that evening one month ago, when I realized too late that I had run out of beer; I could visit my 1995-self and tell him-me to drop out of college and invent Facebook.

But I also have some ethical concerns, which I'd like to share here.

Is to help my other selves in parallel timelines an act of charity, or is it of selfishness?

On the one hand, I'm not profiting in any direct or indirect way from those mariophilanthropic actions. Discounting some enhanced sense of self-satisfaction, they're all genuinely altruistic. On the other hand, the person whom I'm helping isn't really distinct from myself, which could characterize, to put it mildly, nepotism.

Let me ask the same thing in another way: if I were a Christian at Heaven's gate, how would Saint Peter judge my actions? Would he grant me access across the Pearly gates, or would I get a one-way ticket down to the upper hell?

Maybe, I'm deceiving myself with all this self-congratulatory mumbling about time-travel charity, and altruism, and ethics. What matters is that I know that at any moment, one of my parallel selves may drop here in my timeline to help me in some way. And if this is really the case, things start to look less like philanthropy and more like a multiversal freemasonry, with Marios helping Marios across timelines.

Time travel poses so many ethical questions, doesn't it?

(Dear Parallel Me, if you're reading this, let me just make it clear: I favor the Lotto's result over a cold beer.)

The American's Pen and the Soviet's Pencil

"Mme. Secretary, thank you for seeing me" the old, full-bearded man advanced into the office, extending his hand offering a warm handshake.

"Prof. Weisman, what can I do for you?" asked the forty-something-years-old lady with an executive outfit, indicating a seat and showing she wanted to move straight to business.

"Mme. Secretary, you may guess that I'm here to discuss the new budget your administration is drafting," Weisman answered, also going directly to the topic. "My colleagues and I are troubled that the financing of the basic research chairs will be deeply affected under the new rules."

"Prof. Weisman, you know that these are hard times for the economy. We must define priorities…," she didn't mind to complete the argument, judging that it should be self-evident.

More than her words, her body expression, from the rush in the introduction to the clutched hands over the table, made it immediately plain for the man that he didn't have space for negotiation. Clearly, the interview was set only to allow the government to save appearance and to tell later it has been open to discussions.

Nonetheless, Weisman wasn't willing to give up so quickly. The Secretary was a competent manager, but she didn't have any scientific expertise. He decided to profit from his long experience with the science-policy (as well as from his image of lovely grampa) to try to win her to his cause.

"You don't need to tell me, Mme. Secretary," he answered, with an understanding sigh. "Did you know I was a lab assistant in a NASA lab during the Cold war?" he suddenly asked, taking his glasses to clean in his handkerchief.

The Secretary shook her head, wondering how that fact would be relevant in that context.

"You were likely not even born when American astronauts and Soviet cosmonauts found themselves with the odd problem of how to write under zero-G," Weisman continued, now waving a pen as if it was floating. "The ink within the pen's pipe simply didn't obey the patriotic swears neither from one nor from the other. Without a convincing gravitational reason to flow to the pen's ball, it made the simple act of taking notes a hard endeavor," he laughed at the ridiculous of the situation, and she laughed with him too.

"The Americans invested hard on solving this problem: hundred thousand dollars were applied to the research of a pen whose primary goal was to humiliate the Soviets in the conquering of space. For months, NASA commissioned a team to work on this question until they finally came out with an ultramodern ballpoint pen with a triphasic-thermo-fluid self-pumping system able to write not only under zero-G but under any other conditions, even upside down," he paused and asked, "Do you know what the Russians did?"

"Did they developed something similar?" she guessed.

"Not at all. The Russians used a pencil!"

She laughed heartily.

"But is not the story's end," he went on. "The Americans, in their seek for the ideal pen, hired engineers, chemists, and physicists, who focused for months on research lines involving micromechanics, thermodynamics, fluid flow, and composite materials. To support the scientists, a small army of technicians, secretaries, administrators, security officers, drivers, and janitors were hired too. The dollars invested in this project paid not only those people but indirectly reached even the graphic assistant of the publishing house where technical reports were printed, and an illegal Mexican woman, who cleaned the hotel rooms where a specialist's conference took place."

The woman looked entertained with the story.

"The American research money bought vacuum pumps from Pennsylvania, chemicals from North Caroline, precision equipment from New York. After the pen's development, the acquired experience allowed that those scientists and technicians contributed to improving the absorption of drugs in medical treatments and the mechanical control of micro-devices. In fact, this knowledge on microdevices came to be very handy later when a group of researchers spined-off into the private sector to develop personal computers," he said, pointing at her laptop on the desk.

"And about the Russians?" she asked.

"Well, the Russians? The Russians bought a box with twenty-four 2B pencils from a state company near Banska Brystrica, which closed doors when the Slovaks started to import cheaper pencils from China."

The secretary rested in silence for a while. "I see your point, Prof. Weisman," she continued, her tone more conciliatory than at the beginning of the meeting. "Let me propose the following, would you or some of your qualified colleagues seat with my team to reevaluate the budget lines?"

"That's all I could ask for, Mme. Secretary," he answered, standing to shake her hand.

Weisman was already by the door when she asked, "Did it really happen, the story?"

He looked back and answered with a grin, "For all that matters, yes, it did."

The History of My Deaths

Today I complete my mid-life anniversary.

I just got my yearly death-history report from the SSB—the Social Security Bureau. As I commemorate forty-one years old, my death date converged to eighty-two years, with an uncertainty smaller than one year by the first time. That's it: I'll die at eighty-two after "a cardiovascular accident, most probably an aortic rupture."

Many people opt-out and don't get the yearly reports. They prefer to live in the dark about their death dates. Not me. Every year, on my birthday, I anxiously wait for the Bureau message. I carefully check the death chart to compare how it was updated in relation to the last years.

It isn't only an egocentrically morbid curiosity; there are also practical reasons. Knowing my death date allows me to make plans. I know, for instance, given my current investment profile and pension plan, I can retire at sixty-seven, keeping my current income level until my death. And because my death chart sets me as a low-cost client, I pay a health insurance premium about three times lower than that of people who opt-out. Even if my death chart predicted that I may need some intense health treatment in the future, it would still be advantageous to know it, as I could focus my savings on dealing with that.

I know that many people also like to keep their death date private (as recommended by the SSB, by the way). They fear that they may face discrimination, or have problems to get loans, or upset their loved ones, all this stuff. I used to worry about these things as well. But now that my death date converged, and I know that my mid-life is in the normal range of my demographics, I don't care anymore.

This is the reason for this post. I'll make my death chart public for the first time!

It still amazes me how actuarial sciences evolved in the last years. As a nonspecialist, I read a lot to understand the principles of their predictions. It goes much beyond traditional Bayesian inference, into deep-learning AI fed by tons of socio-psychological-genetic data.

You know, there are dozens of apps that allow yourself to simulate death-charts. But they are far away from the accuracy from those issued by the SSB. The Bureau has the most advanced algorithms and access to the most complete database. They know your DNA, they know your health history, they keep track of your consumption habits, they build your psychological profile out of your social network interactions. The SSB crosses data with all other government agencies. They have access to your driving history, tax declarations, civil procedures.

The SSB death charts became so precise that when they tell me that I will die at eighty-two plus-minus one, I don't dispute that. I know that's bound to happen.

Well, within 90% of chances. There are the residuals: two percent of chances that I'll live longer; and eight percent that I'll die before. And how detailed the death chart is! My residuals discriminate 4% chances for stroke at about 60 years old, 1% for traffic-related accidents, 0.2% for abdominal cancer, 0.03% for "suicide following depression at the 55-60 age range," <0.001% for airplane accidents.

Of course, I'm not silly, I try to improve my odds. Since my death date started to converge to about eighty years, I've been running many death-chart simulations trying to stretch my lifespan.

Less meat, more exercise; electing a conservative parliament, electing a progressist president; moving to the mountains, taking holidays at the beach: I've tested so many variables, none made any statistically significant difference.

Running a life-span optimizer, I discovered, however, that a seven figures salary and a daughter (why not a son? it escapes me) could shift my death date ahead by two or three years. Now I just must convince my boss and my wife :)

But I'm starting to blab. At this rhythm, I'll die before finishing this post…

Then, here it goes. As promised, my death chart goes public:

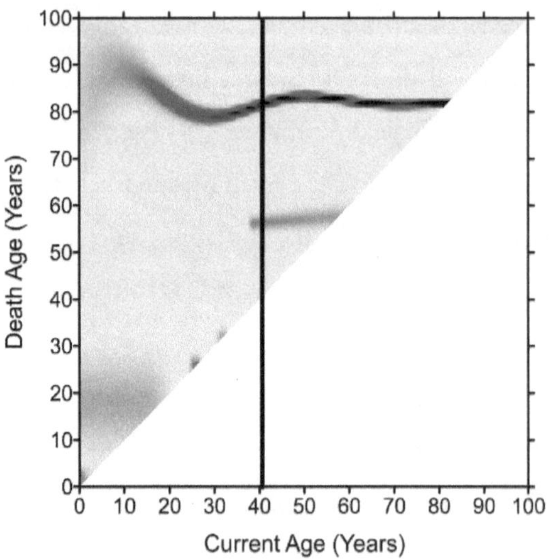

Exciting, isn't it?

You see, year by year in the horizontal axis, from zero to forty-one how my death-history evolved. You see from forty-two on how it should evolve. Of course, the next years' predictions will be Bayesianly updated, and I'll get them on my upcoming birthdays from the SSB's messages.

I really like to analyze my death chart. It helps to understand my life; the paths I've chosen and those I've abandoned.

See that soft death-cloud when I was a teen? That's typical for males between sixteen and twenty-two. We have strong bodies and half-matured brains. That's a recipe for disaster. That's the reason people often say, "don't trust anyone under thirty." Naturally, I survived that death peak.

That another little sharp peak when I was twenty-six? That was my military service term in the middle east. It appeared for the first time in my twenty-five-years-old SSB report, right after I received the notice that I'd be deployed. I still remember myself trembling, looking at the bump in the chart as if it were a tumor in a biopsy.

The shadow at thirty-two? I was sent to Rio for one year as a company's representative for Latin America. It turned out it was a pleasant time, and I came back alive.

Since a couple of years ago, the chart started to show a soft ridge for "death due to stroke at the later fifties." I don't know the reason it showed up only now. What am I doing wrong? Nothing to be especially alarmed about, according to my physician. But it seems that the SSB knows me better than myself anyway.

Remember the terror-attack wave about ten years ago? Everyone panicking about those coward bastards blowing trains and shopping malls. Yet, no sign of that on my death chart. The danger was overestimated by public opinion, sensationalist media, and slander politicians.

Despite all that ado, the terror attacks never increased my death chances.

And that's also a lesson for all those people afraid of checking their death charts: only they don't know them. Everyone else—companies, banks, politicians, government— know our death charts with more or less accuracy. And they use that info all the time for the better or worse. Anyone who doesn't check her own death chart is just putting herself at a disadvantage.

For now, that's it. But before I finish, I'd like to thank you all beforehand for all mid-life greetings.

The Statistician's Love Life

Son, it's time to tell you the story of how your mother and I met.

It starts seventeen years ago during my bachelor's times. I'd just graduated, and I knew that, as a statistician, my chances with girls weren't the best. Anyway, I was bold enough to guess that I would be able to date ten girls, who would eventually take me as a husband. My problem was to decide which of these ten would be "the one."

If I just got married to the first girl, probably one of the other nine would have been a better choice for me. If I waited till the last one to be able to compare all of them, I wouldn't get a second chance with any of the earlier nine girls.

But I had a degree in mathematics, it should do me some good.

I knew that after each date, I would be able to rank the girl in comparison to all the others that I dated before. Of course, I wouldn't know anything about the next girls, who I could still date in the future.

It was a classical mathematical problem: the best solution is well known from the Optimal Stopping theory. I had only to date and discard the first $10/e$ girls and, then, to get married to the first one who was ranked better than any of my earlier dates. (*e*, you remember, is the base of the natural logarithms, about 2.718.)

Then, that was precisely what I did. I decided to never call again any of the first $10/e$, that is about 4 dates.

I confess that it was quite hard to resist girl number two. But I knew, math was working for me. I didn't call her again. As I also didn't call back, girls number three and four.

In the next summer, I was only stress. I knew that now that the game was afoot: any of my next dates could be my companion for life!

Girl number five was disappointing. Number six was fine, but not better than my number two. (Damn it! I still missed her.)

Then, in the winter, I dated girl number seven.

Son, she was amazing! Beautiful, intelligent, funny; also a mathematician! I had no doubt: she scored higher than any of the previous six girls (maybe even higher than number two).

I proposed and, for my delight, she accepted. We got married in the next summer.

This was how I met your mother.

Why does she live with that other guy today?

Well, it turns out to be that I was still her number five.

The End and the Life

"Past time is finite, future time is infinite." E. Hubble.

"Everything has returned: Sirius and the spider, and your thoughts at this hour, and your thought that everything returns." F. Nietzsche.

Friedrich didn't wait for the answer; the conclusion drew itself evident to him. He said, "If the universe collapses, then it wouldn't have time to give birth to your wonderful semi-eternal beings. If besides, the universe evolves through recurring cycles of expansion and collapse, then we are possibly talking about the eternal return. You know, with the same events repeating over and over again."

Edwin didn't agree, "The incredibly high temperatures at the beginning of the expansion would certainly give rise to different histories within each cycle. And even if for some unknown reason, all initial conditions at the beginning of each expansion were the same, quantum fluctuations would quickly create divergent histories. I can't see how eternal return could take place."

"No, you didn't get my point," Friedrich protested. "I'm not expecting to come back to existence in every cycle. Consider, however, that I'm talking about an infinite number of expansions and collapses. Take ten to any power that you wish. After an amazingly large number of cycles, it's sure that not only all the initial conditions but also the quantum fluctuations will be by pure chance the same as those of the cycle that we are living right now.

"This means that every single feature of the history of that universe will be exactly like ours: the solar system will emerge, Earth will condense, life will be born. All creatures will evolve following precisely the same descendent line that brought us here.

"This also means that we had exactly this same talk in this same room infinite times before, and we will have it countless times more. Is that a curse?" he joked.

Edwin couldn't disagree anymore. The idea was far-fetched, but whenever you take the infinite as a partner, the inconceivable turns into trivial. He also knew that Friedrich's speculation rested on a cyclic-universe hypothesis. Take it out, and things would go very differently: "Now, Friedrich, just suppose that instead of cycles, the universe will really go on expanding forever. What's your best bet for the future in this case?"

"Absolute darkness," Friedrich answered at once. "Given enough time, all the stars will be burnt; even the black holes will have evaporated through quantum emissions. Entropy will be at the maximum, the temperature will be the same everywhere. The universe will be completely lifeless.”

“Dark, I agree; lifeless not,” Edwin provoked. “Vacuum fluctuations will still forever be a remaining source of free energy in the universe, and life will feast on it.”

The idea immediately captured Friederich’s attention. Edwin continued, “Fueled by these fluctuations, molecules will slowly move in the ethereal residual clouds between the dead stars, colliding with each other now and then. And if in one of these collisions a photon is emitted quickly enough, a new stable molecule can even appear.

“Naturally, a simple chemical reaction that takes place within a fraction of a second on Earth will take millions of years to happen in the heat-dead universe. But all that the universe will have in abundance by then is time, isn’t it?”

“Well, at least until the protons start to decay,” warned Friedrich.

Without mind the interruption, Edwin went on, “It doesn’t matter how improbable it is; it’s just a matter of waiting for it. More and more complex molecules will form in the vacuum until one day one of them will get to the point that it will be able to self-catalyze. At that moment buried in the forgotten future, life will reborn, but on absolutely unthinkable time scales.

"Playing eons as seconds, the concentration of this self-catalyzing molecule will grow. Eventually, one of its daughters will make a wrong copy of itself and branch into a new species. These species will compete and arm-race against each other for the scarce resources. They will evolve following the same Darwinian tools as it happened in the warm universe so many times before.

"They will evolve, and one day, they will become conscious of themselves and of their dark universe. With their frozen semi-eternal bodies, they will cry for their dead and maybe tell their children about the hero who once spent half of his life trying to go back home after a long battle.

"One day, they will even theorize that in an infinitesimal instant of time—the first trillion years—the universe was full of stars."

Friedrich was wondering about the frozen semi-eternal beings when the obvious question struck him. "Edwin, your scenario would only happen if the universe expanded forever. What would happen if by any chance it came to a collapse?" he asked.

He didn't wait for the answer; the conclusion drew itself evident to him. Friedrich said,

The Borderless Truth

The problem with religions is that they are too simple. Creation of the universe and of life, the relationship between gods and men, the fate of everything; for all those issues, religions give trivial answers. These aren't old woman's grumbles. These are convictions I've borne with me for the best of my eighty years. My children and grandchildren never wasted their time in a church; I hope my coming great-grandchild won't do, too.

Sometimes, religious questions even look complex, but transubstantiation, miracles, soul-body relation, the paradox between God's omniscience and human's free will are only philosophical dramas when hold by scholastic hands of theologians with all their affection for circular and hermetic reasoning.

Upon scrutiny, however, the most elaborate rituals and lifelong sacerdotal dedications only disguise trivialities, dressing them as exoteric wisdom. The most involved analysis of the most rigorous Cabalist will only reveal formulas already known, maybe with new pompous words.

And it gets even worse down the road: the faith of the simple layman does not care about those metaphysical elucubrations. It is only a matter of invoking magic powers of divine beings, and everything is possible, even the impossible.

Then, here is my question: religions are simple, too simple for my taste. Everything under their magic lenses is easy to understand. And this is by itself paradoxical: is it not contradictory that the world, with its infinite multiplicity of things, facts, and relations, could be so trivially explained?

This embarrassing mediocrity of the religions mirrors the finitude of the individuals. Their fallible memories, their limited reasoning and language, their short life spans make impossible to build any explanation minimally worth of the complexity of the universe.

But it is not entirely correct that there are no exceptions among the religions. There is one that stands out and works to overcome the limitations of individual beings. Its followers have been spread around the world for centuries, maybe millennia. Each one of these individuals, far from knowing a complete system of myths and rituals, only know an infinitesimal part of that his religion as a whole knows. Most of the time, this infinitesimal part corresponds to the efforts of an entire life of dedication and study.

No one of these individuals knows the entire religious truth. They couldn't know it even if they wished to do so.

Maybe, if a lifespan were counted in centuries, not in years, and if memory did not succumb under the weight of thousands of libraries, then a single priest would be able to grasp a bit more than an infinitesimal of their religion.

The complexity of that system is so imposing that many followers do not even know that they are holders of religious knowledge. Unpretentious hosts, they only pass this knowledge ahead.

Generation after generation, thousands of priests meditate, follow rituals, and teach. Even when two of them occasionally join into a discussion, they only lose themselves in a borderless labyrinth of contradictory and confusing reflections, as their knowledge only holds meaning when seen as a whole, which is just impossible for them.

I admire these determined, however, blind priests. But if no concrete knowledge, no moral lesson, no spiritual comfort can be derived from their religion, why do they still nurture and teach it?

I'm not religious. But I have an early memory, from seven decades ago, of a rare public sermon of a grand-priest. I was a child surrounded by the immense stone cathedral. The feeling of the cold air smelling burnt incense is still vivid in me. The old man climbed to the gothic pulpit and taught "The Parable of the Ant." Maybe it is the only religious sermon that has ever made sense to me.

The Parable of the Ant

Silence! Who are you to tell what the ONE-ALL-MIGHT can do? When within your most deep meanness was born your belief that you can delve into His will? Do not you know that He is not only bigger than you deem but also bigger than anything that you will ever be able to deem? Fall on your face to the ground, as only it may teach you about your littleness. Learn the only truth that fits you: humble yourself into your bewilderment.

How can the ant challenge the destruction of her offspring? How can she challenge the goals of the ONE-LARGER-THAN-ALL? How can she probe into the Good and the Evil, given the little that she can peruse around herself?

If she cannot even behold the stem where she climbs and the leaves that sprout from it, how can she curse the day in which she was born or the world that shows itself bitter? How can the ant ask about the wisdom that rules her fate, if she does not know anything about the shrub that feeds her? Shrub that is only another one among hundreds on the farm! Farm that she cannot even suppose to be, even less to guess that it is only one single farm among hundreds of others that fill hundreds of markets that feed thousands of beings. Beings so much bigger than herself that her sight could not reach their upper edges. Then, how can the ant rule the fall of the righteous or the death of the innocent to be right or wrong?

Do not start you, as those whose the faith is ill and weak, to moan about love and pity. How can you believe that the ONE-ALL-THE-SAME would submit Himself unto such feelings, maybe worth of petty frail beings, but all unworthy of whom who is everything? Do you think that law, tenderness, honor, pity would have any bearing in His wholeness?

Ah, Ant! You cannot even behold the stem, what about the market!

Guard my words. I, who already wandered for the whole land, can tell you: all your beliefs are false. You live your stainless life waiting for His blessing; you join your people in prayers, carols, holocausts, and alms. Do you really believe that the ONE-IN-EVERYWHERE would be bribed by those pitiful deeds? Do you believe that He would diminish Himself into a paltry judge weighing your vices and virtues?

If someday you come unto His nearness, know that it shall not be because you lived in this or that way. Shall not dare to guess His aims! All that you must to do is to muffle in voice and thoughts, and to live for the Glory of the ONE-ALL-KNOWLEDGE.

THE LAST DIGIT OF INFINITY

1.

The universe is a simulation; every kid learns that in high school. It is just part of pop culture. As much surprising this discovery was, with all its profound philosophical and moral implications, it never really caused much commotion. The discovery itself was never a state secret: it quickly made the news before any silly bureaucrat could think of quarantining it.

A.

Paul O. tried to put himself together. Still shaking and sweating, he rambled nervously around the living room, avoiding looking back at the naked blond woman on the sofa. Her sweet and delicate perfume was, however, a wearing remind of her presence.

With his heart pounding, he breathed deeply and slowly to calm down. He tried to take his mind out of the room by invoking elements of the Simulation theory. These routine thoughts have always helped him relax in stressful situations. They were his comfort zone: for years he had been teaching the topic in his introduction to quantum sciences for senior high school. Moreover, he enjoyed the pleasant feeling that someone else was ultimately responsible for his actions; even knowing well that it was only a self-deception.

These were soothing thoughts, but not so much this time. His mind was flooded with recalls of the woman's warm silky skin in his hands and her inquisitive blue eyes reaching deep into him. And those feelings overpowered any silly mind exercise.

2.

The universe overflow was discovered right after the release of the third generation of quantum computers. Mathematicians aimed at breaking a new record for the number of computed digits of π, when they stumbled across something disturbingly unexpected: after a very long sequence of uniformly-distributed digits, π digits flowed in periodic sequences, over and over again, with a sharply skewed distribution.

They quickly realized that the problem was not on π itself, this exact feature was found in every tested irrational. The problem was on the underlying mathematical operations to compute extremely large numbers. After certain limit in the quantum memory, every additional operation returned the same periodic sequence of digits. The universe was in overflow. It was just like when an old four-digit mechanical counter reached 9999 and then started over with 0000.

When this discovery reached the public, it was received with relative indifference. Confidently hooked to their scientific ignorance, most people did not grasp the implicit meaning of the universe overflow.

B.

Finally, Paul O. started to relax. He breathed normally again and, between confusing thoughts, he even appreciated the elegantly decorated flat. He could certainly live in such clean, bright, white-beige spacious rooms. The place was in complete silence. He walked to what seemed to be the woman's sleeping room at the end of the corridor, still without looking at her on the white sofa.

He never really felt under control of external forces for being a simulation. He just liked to play with that thought. Now and then he heard of a suicide attributed to simulation depressive disorder, but he was pretty sure that those people would have found another reason to end their lives anyway; just like people praying for the

Simulators in mystical cults would have found some other silliness to believe in.

Paul O. examined the live 3D picture on the wall above the bed. It was a life-size interactive portrait of the woman. She was a stunning blond, maybe in the early thirties like him. It was difficult to know her age for sure. Given the high standard of her flat, she could easily afford fancy bio-makeups. In principle, she could be a couple of decades older than her look.

He was still astonished that such a high-score woman had accepted to go on a physical date with him, let alone to invite him home. He knew he was somewhat charming in the virtual rooms, but his profile never scored more than the average. He definitely had no idea what he had done so right that time to attract her.

In the live picture, she wore a red dress and stood in a sunny green spring background. A lavender aroma matched the scene. The portrait looked at him; it had been set up to engage with anyone in the room. It was the same intense look that had forced him to deviate his eyes while talking to her earlier in the evening. Suddenly, she smiled at him warmly and joyfully. "Gosh, you're gorgeous," Paul O. surprised himself murmuring to the picture.

The woman's red dress, in sharp contrast against the green field and the white decoration of the room, generously revealed her amazing body. Her firm breasts hanging naturally under the dress, the light shadows sculpting her nipples, her fair skin emerging tight from within the red cotton, everything in her figure excited him. His blood burned, and his penis twitched. He wanted to go back to her.

He shut his eyes, trying to focus again on his relaxing thoughts. He leaned against the dresser, his palms supporting his weight, and rested for a long moment.

3.

No matter the physical nature of the quantum computer or the number of giga-qubytes available in the memory, no arithmetic is possible above the so-called Ω constant. Ω is one of those vast quantities defying the imagination and the metaphors; but it is far, far away smaller than ridiculously large numbers mathematicians have been conceptually playing with for centuries, like those in Graham's class.

The universe overflow has always been deemed as a quantum property. However, there is no way to know whether arithmetic based on classical states would also overflow. It is just not possible to assemble a classical computer with enough memory to test it, not at least without using all atoms of the planet to build up such a device.

Many tried to rationalize the universe overflow as a physics law, just like the universe pixelization caused by Heisenberg's principle. But the mainstream scientific community soon recognized in the weird periodic sequence of skewed-distributed digits what came to be the most bizarre, astonishing discovery science ever did: the universe was a simulation.

The universe overflow was clearly a "glitch in the matrix," to stick to a popular metaphor. Many other glitches had been found since then. They are always connected to inconsistencies in large quantum systems as if the responsible for the universe simulation assigned a fair, but a limited amount of maximum memory that could be allocated in pure quantum states in our universe. This amount is big enough to smoothly run what we understand as natural processes but too small to fool smart mathematicians within the simulation.

Several philosophers have pointed out the historical irony: thousands of years ago Pythagoreans tried to hide the existence of irrational numbers from the public; they saw them as an essential flaw in their conception of a perfect universe. Now, the impossibility of computing true irrational numbers revealed that the universe was not even real.

C.

Paul O. remembered the interview with a pop-star physicist he had watched last night. (Or was it last year? Last night strangely felt like some distant past.) The scientist had drawn an interesting comparison between the role of irrational numbers in ancient Greek culture and in the discovery of the quantum overflow. Paul O. wished he had thought of that himself. This was precisely the kind of keen reasoning he was never able to come up with.

4.

The popularization of the Simulation theory never had a significant impact on the quotidian. It did not result in any new technology or product. At most, it provided a physical background to the anthropic principle and explained why the cosmos is not in a coherent quantum state. These are hardly discoveries that would ever impact any layperson's life.

The Simulation theory was a praised curiosity; a matter for superficial debates in virtual salons. Every year there were a number of incidents around the world attributed to it, and nowadays, the psychiatric community recognizes *simulation depressive disorder* as a condition affecting a minor fraction of the population. Beyond that, most people just kept going with their lives as usual.

Academy briefly saw a surge of people enrolled in math and philosophy courses. Many cults deifying "the Simulators" sprang as well, but they were never trendy. The main religions went through some denial period, but excepting some most conservative sects, they adapted well. After all, they keep their theologians in the payroll to do this oily magic.

Nevertheless, the Simulation theory strongly impacted culture, especially after it made its way into the school programs. The number of cultural products connected to it is just uncountable (although uncountable is a word that may not mean so much anymore).

D.

How many times The Matrix was re-shot? Paul O. was asking himself. He still fancied the original movie with Keanu Reeves as the best. All remakes, especially the interactive ones, had lost pace with too many special effects and fight scenes.

Most of fictional productions exploring the Simulation theory that he had recently watched were just silly anthropocentric entertainment: the Simulators were depicted either as gods playing with humans, or machines feeding on humans, or humans simulating their own history, as if the universe—still glorious in spite of its downgraded status—revolved around humans. He always tried to emphasize this point with his students.

A sudden motion in a small live picture on the dresser brought him back from his thoughts. Paul O. looked at this other portrait of the blond woman and thought of her lying naked on the sofa in the other room. He was angry at himself. He knew the feeling well. He was tired of these waves of emotions coming and going, blurring his judgment.

He walked to the bathroom just out of the sleeping room and washed his face and her perfume from him. He could not stay longer.

5.

Despite many hypotheses, no one has any idea about who or what is responsible for the universe simulation; or even less why they have been running the simulation in the first place. Obviously, it is immaterial to speculate whether the Simulators are aware of (or care about) our awareness. These topics have entirely remained out of the scientific scrutiny, as a matter of endless philosophical debates.

Different thinkers have proposed that the universe overflow is likely a flag left hidden on purpose in the cosmos' structure so that any civilization in the universe advanced enough to uncover it could be aware of their condition of simulated beings. A group of scientists has even raised funds to create a beacon to try, still unsuccessfully, contacting the Simulators.

Most of the contemporary philosophers agree that despite the profound ontological and epistemological implications, the Simulation theory does not have a significant impact on ethics. As long as there is no evidence of direct interference of the Simulators on our realm, our universe still works as a closed system ruled by well-defined physical laws, with living beings evolving by selection processes, and societies following their own historical courses.

It is not surprising that every attempt of invoking the Simulation theory as a mitigation factor in the legal sphere has always been immediately dismissed.

E.

Paul O. was awfully tired. There was nothing he could do about the woman in the other room. It was always the same feeling of regret and shame—and he loathed himself also for that. It was time to go home.

He walked back into the living room; his back arched and his eyes down as if to avoid contact with hers. In silence, he crossed the room straight to the exit. Only after feeling safe by gripping the cold doorknob, he looked back at her. The dark brown-bluish marks carved into the woman's neck, where his hands had strangled her, creepily smiled at him as a second mouth.

He sounded sincere and sorrow when he whispered to the dead body before leaving: "Don't mind, gorgeous. This is just a simulation."

PARABLES OF THE MEN

The Man in the Stone Tower: Instinct

I.

Adam was awakened by a cold and dry scratch running up his naked thigh. He didn't think twice, he threw whatever the thing was away and immediately crushed it with a rock. Getting to himself, he examined the smashed creature, with its long, legless bleeding body covered by overlapping scales.

He was especially impressed by the small triangular head and the forked tong. He had never seen anything like that before, but the sharp pair of fangs certainly looked threatening.

In fact, it's not only that he had never seen such a creature. He had never seen anything moving by itself before. Maybe there was a unique exception, in a time so distant in the past that it mixed with his dreams.

He couldn't sleep that night anymore. He remained on his soft-soil nest looking at the cloudy dark sky, wondering whether there were other things like that moving anywhere.

II.

Adam's days were always the same. He would wake up at the first light, eat from the tree, drink from the narrow river, and start his work, pushing the stone blocks up in the construction site to build the tower.

After hours of labor, with his legs burning from exhaustion, Adam would sit at the tower's highest edge, looking at the landscape. Apart from the incomplete construction beneath him, there was nothing particularly noticeable around. The flat gray desert extended to the horizon in all directions, until it met the also invariably gray and cloudy sky.

From above, he could see the tree that fed him. He could also see the narrow river, which stretched in smooth curves, splitting the landscape in two. Besides that, all that remained were the scattered rectangular rock blocks, which he gathered to build the tower.

The tower was a pyramidal structure, made of juxtaposed blocks and sided by a spiraling path left on recessed stones, on where new rocks were pushed up. Seen from a distance, the tower looked like an immense triangular hill, halfway built, with the first stones being assembled to yield the next layer.

Nobody had ever told Adam what to do. And he hadn't started the tower himself either. The construction had been already there when he arrived, and it was clear to him from the beginning that his goal was to continue it, laying new stone layers. No training was ever needed. He felt clear as hungry the things he had to do. He knew how to choose the proper rocks for each part of the construction, as naturally as he knew the color of the edible fruits in the tree.

Adam had no idea how long he had been building the tower. He had no memories from a previous time, and he couldn't tell the laborious gray days apart.

III.

Every day, as soon as the sky started to darken, Adam would check the daily progress on the latest stones. Despite the fatigue, the work in the tower gave him a sense of fulfillment, maybe even of purpose. He would walk down, eat from the tree, and drink from the river. Then, he would lie down on his spot of soft soil and sleep a dreamless night.

But sometimes, he dreamt. He could see himself, or at least a version of himself, small and skinny, walking along the narrow river towards the distant half-built pyramidal construction standing alone in the desert. A figure walked in his direction; a tall and muscular man, like himself. The man also followed the narrow river but coming from the tower. When they crossed each other, the man looked curiously at him and, without stopping, grunted something sounding like "adm."

This was a recurrent dream. In fact, this was his only dream, maybe his only early memory from a pre-tower age. He never bothered to know what that word the man said meant, but he got used to thinking of himself as Adam.

Awaken after such a dream; he would wonder whether there were indeed other people like him. And if so, where are their towers and their trees? Do they drink from the same river? Who and where are those who had started his own tower and had left it unfinished for him? But those thoughts and questions would die as fast as he fell back asleep.

IV.

Few nights after he smashed the threatening moving creature with a rock, Adam dreamt again. But this time, it was an entirely new dream.

He felt a cold and dry scratch on his thigh, and before he could shake the thing out, the scratch felt silky and pleasant. In the dark, the creature wasn't the long threatening animal anymore; she was like him. Like him but different. She was soft and warm. And his body responded to hers as it never did to anything else. They embraced each other to become one. Adam felt drowning in an ecstasy of entirely unknown feelings. He was suddenly awakened by a carnal explosion of pleasure and, for a moment, searched for her as if she were real.

That night he couldn't sleep anymore too. He knew his work at the tower was over. He felt—he knew—he had a new purpose. At the first light, he glanced up at the unfinished tower by the last time and walked away following the narrow river.

Not much long after he started his trip, Adam saw someone coming in his way, also following the narrow river, but in the opposite direction. It was a person like him, but smaller and skinnier; a boy. He looked at the boy, and for the first time in his life, something made sense. When they crossed each other, he managed to grunt the only word he knew, while the boy looked confused and shy. Although curious, Adam didn't stop. All he wanted now was to meet her, the silky, warm Eve from his latest dream.

He continued walking along the narrow river and didn't even notice when the tower disappeared below the horizon behind him.

The Man in the Ivory Tower: Reason

The Construction of the Ivory Tower

Kamal was the oldest son of a wealthy merchant of the village of Roch. Since a young age, he was famous for his bright mind, already mastering all arts and sciences, while other kids at his age barely could speak. He grew up to become a respected scholar, known in the whole land.

When his father died, he alone inherited all the family's fortune, as it was the law.

What he did next surprised even those who always took him for an eccentric scholastic: he decided to build an ivory tower, to isolate himself from mundane distractions, and solve every natural and human problems he judged to be outstanding. Why the tower had to be made of ivory, nobody ever found out.

The tower construction, with all provisions he would need for a life in there, revealed to be extremely expensive. It consumed most of Kamal's wealth. The little that rested, he donated to his brothers and sisters, granting them certain comfort, but far below what they were used to.

The tower sprouted in an isolated spot in the central plain, equidistant from the village of Roch, the holy city of Vacan, the great city of Oir'yn, the conjoined cities of J'lem and G'zar, and the forest of Amzan. Following the detailed projects of Kamal, the best masons, carpenters, builders, and architects from Oir'yn gave shape to the tower, working on the massive amount of ivory imported from Amzan.

The tower grew impeccably white, as a solid five-faced polygonal structure. It looked like a monolithic pentagonal regular rod, almost without any particular structure or decoration. Its only remarkable features were the crenelations on the terrace parapet and the five small windows, one on each face of the highest floor, where Kamal had his apartment built.

Although Kamal's apartment took the whole floor, it contained only a small bed and a work desk laid in the middle of the ample pentagonal space illuminated through the five windows. The floors below stocked everything he would need for the next years of work and solitude. At a corner of his apartment, a set of spiral stairs communicated to the floors below and the tower terrace above.

In the days immediately before the ivory tower was finished, Kamal moved to his apartment in there. The masons were instructed to seal the only entrance, as he was not supposed to leave, or anyone to enter until his work was accomplished.

As the workers left, silence waved through the tower. Kamal's endeavor was about to start.

The First Challenge

In his first night alone, Kamal climbed to the tower's terrace and contemplated the darkness between the stars. He mused about the mysteries of the universe.

Back to his apartment, he sat at his work desk and thought of the first challenge ahead of him, to derive a final theory of everything.

For years he worked till he found the solution. He finally arrived at a formulation that could conciliate quantum mechanics and general relativity, even in divergent limits near event horizons and at the Big Bang. In Kamal's theory, it was clear why the universe was born in a low entropy state, how it evolved into galactic clusters, and why it was on an accelerating expansion.

Then, Kamal derived a new formulation of classical and quantum mechanics based on the evolution of ensembles. Entropy and time irreversibility were naturally incorporated at the microscopic level, having time-reversible trajectories as particular limits. In his theory, the time arrow wasn't a mystery anymore, and quantum evolution from pure into mixed states followed a natural path, eliminating the measurement problem.

Kamal was satisfied, but a lot more work waited for him.

The Second Challenge

In the next day, Kamal stood at the window facing the holy city of Vacan. He looked at the maze of buildings and their thin minarets, surrounding the immense golden cathedral. He observed the constant flow of pilgrims converging into the city's inner walls for their prayers. He thought of how deluded they were, wasting their time and hopes with false idols.

Kamal knew that even the most eloquent proof of the nonexistence of Vacan's divinities wouldn't change the minds of those faithful people. The better he could do was to show that there was nothing magical or supernatural about life and the human soul, and hope that the kids of the next generations would be brighter than their parents to appreciate that truth. With these thoughts in mind, it was time to tackle his second challenge, to derive a theory of life and mind.

Again, for years Kamal worked till he found the solution. He first showed how life originated on Earth, through a sequence of prebiotic self-catalytic processes fed by the sun and supported by inorganic mineral nanostructures. He showed how these processes increased in complexity and autonomy, purely following natural selection processes, without any divine intervention, up to the first autonomous mono-cellular being was born.

Then, he turned to the other extreme of the problem. He unveiled how the mind was an emergent phenomenon arising from brain activity. He proved that this activity was expressed in layers: a first unconscious proto-self merely registering deviations from the organism homeostasis; a core conscience creating representative images of the proto-self; and an autobiographical-self binding the core-conscience history through memories and forecasts. Kamal's theory definitively proved how emotions, feelings, memories, reason, and consciousness emanate from this process, without the need of invoking an extra-corporeal soul.

Kamal was satisfied, but to unveil the mysteries of the universe, life, and soul was easy. The hard challenges were still ahead.

The Third Challenge

Early in the next day, Kamal stood at the window facing the great city of Oir'yn. It challenged his eyes with its metropolitan complexity. At its center, an island of tall crystal towers where the beautiful people of Oir'yn lived punched the sky. The towers were surrounded by an immense circle of wood slums where the poor people of Oir'yn lived. He saw that division and thought of how unfair it was. It was time to work on his third challenge: to derive a new social contract.

Kamal worked for years till he accomplished it. There were three problems to tackle: economic growth, which granted the wealth of society as a whole; inequality, which was source of social instability and low quality of life of the poor people of Oir'yn; and heritage, which for centuries rendered the children of the beautiful people of the city an unfair advantage over the children of the poor people, in their future competition for the best opportunities.

First, he focused on the economic growth problem. He devised a market regulatory system to raise productivity through stimulating free initiative, infrastructure development, and stable institutions. He established the optimal balance between macroeconomic variables, to reach monetary stability, but maximizing employment and economic expansion.

As for the inequality problem, he redesigned the tax system discouraging over-concentration of wealth. He refocused the city's savings investments on universalization of social security and basic infrastructure. He proposed new political institutions to forge democratic stability, where the power of corporative lobbies was tempered down. He created certification seals to stimulate consumption of products out of fair-work conditions.

Finally, he tackled the heritage problem. Kamal wrote rules to professionalize access to public jobs, eliminating nepotism. Then, he remodeled the educational system, making it universal. A new pedagogy was developed to optimize learning and creativity, by tailoring communication and content not only to different ages but also to different psychological profiles. He redesigned the school progression system to identify and award skills.

Kamal was happy and ready to move to his next challenge.

The fourth Challenge

In the next morning, Kamal was awakened by an explosion. He looked through the window facing the conjoined cities of J'lem and G'zar in time to see a dense column of black smoke rising from a bombing in the central market of G'zar. A swarm of arrows shot from G'zar draw a nasty dark parabola in the sky before falling on J'lem. The nightmare scenario was completed by high-intensity red-laser blasts from J'sem diffracting in the smoke before burning most of the arrows.

Kamal wondered about how irrational that war had been being. Resting for centuries, no one in either city could tell the real reasons for the fight anymore. When asked about, they would blame the other side, resorting to nonsensical tails of millennial rights granted by ancestral prophets. The truth was the war had become their way of living. The economy of both cities revolved around it, and generation after generation, their leaders had become comfortable with that cruel, unstable balance.

It was time to face the next challenge, to reach a peace agreement between the two cities.

For the next years, Kamal worked on that. He drew terms for the fairest land partition and share of resources. He proposed economic reforms to allow a transition from a war into a cooperative economy. He designed new justice institutions, amnesty conditions, diplomatic protocols, and intercultural actions, targeting at healing ages of mutual hate.

Kamal was satisfied. A new challenge awaited.

The Fifth Challenge

In the next day, Kamal looked at the forest of Amzan. He knew the forest was in danger. For years in the tower, he had observed how people from all land had been keeping their lifestyle through a savage exploration of energy and raw materials from the forest. To his amazement, the people-of-the-forest readily helped in this process, without even noticing that they had been impoverishing themselves.

Kamal mourned the loss of billions of years of stored information with each extinct species. Even worse, the forest was essential for regulating the climate of the land, and by destroying it, a real risk of disrupting the food production was on the horizon.

Kamal knew what he had to do. Then, for years, he worked on the way to balance current economic needs, future ecological demands, and the well-being of the people-of-the-forest. He developed a new energetic matrix based on renewable sources to reduce the impact on the forest. He invented new photovoltaic organic polymers for multiple-ending solar-energy harvesting. Then, he synthesized efficient water-splitting photocatalytic agents for massive chemical energy storage.

He also designed a sustainable model for the forest exploration, fairly incorporating the workforce of the people-of-the-forest. Finally, he designed efficient recycling chains and created the means to clearly account for externalities into the commodities' price.

Once more, Kamal was satisfied. Only one more challenge remained: death.

The Final Challenge

In the next morning, Kamal felt homesick. He thought of his beloved father, who had died from devastating cancer; and of his youngest brother, who had succumbed to malaria during a business trip to Amzan. With the slow steps of an old man, Kamal walked to the window facing his village, Roch.

It was time to tackle his final challenge: death.

In the next years, Kamal worked on ways to cure the main diseases afflicting people everywhere in the land. He started with malaria, which was surprisingly easy to deal with. He developed genetically modified malaria-free mosquitos to replace the original vector population and an efficient recombinant vaccine. Cancer was much challenging. But Kamal ingeniously engineered a virus able to detect proteins over-expressed in tumors. Inertly spread in the body; these viruses were activated only when such detection was positive. Then, they would kill the cell by disrupting its metabolic cycle.

Kamal developed drugs to regenerate circulatory system in arteriosclerosis, self-adapting vaccines against flu, genetic therapies to eliminate insulin's cellular resistance in diabetes, therapeutic viruses to clean up the brain from the excess of beta-amyloid peptides in Alzheimer.

But Kamal knew that even if he were given a new lifetime, he wouldn't be able to find the cure for every possible illness. Then, he drew plans for sustainable and independent funding of medical research, which at his time was in the hands of Oir'yn corporations, with little incentive to develop procedures and drugs beyond market interests.

This time, Kamal wasn't entirely satisfied, but he conceded that this was the best he could do.

The Collapse of the Ivory Tower

Kamal had finally completed his self-imposed mission. Decades before he had set to himself the goal of solving all problems of nature, society, and men. He finally did it to the best of his efforts. It cost him a lifetime of solitude. He never took a wife or had children. But he thought it was entirely worth it. Now it was time to leave the ivory tower and make his achievements public.

He climbed to the terrace to ask for help. He needed masons to come and break the tower's entrance seal.

He stood at the side facing Roch, his village, and waved. His brothers and sisters, who still kept a grudge against him for having wasted the family's wealth, decided to ignore his calls.

Then, he faced the holy city of Vacan and waved. The priests saw him from the golden cathedral but decided to ignore him too. They knew he was an atheist with heretic ideas about man and his immortal, holy soul. They scolded him and convinced the pilgrims that he was an iconoclast sent by the devil to destroy their faith. Vacan didn't answer his calls.

Kamal went to the wall facing the great city of Oir'yn and waved. The beautiful people of the city saw him from their crystal towers, but also decided to ignore his calls. They knew of Kamal's pretension of reforming the city and were not happy with that. They ridiculed him and convinced the poor people of the city that he was a traitor sent by enemy nations to destroy their homeland. Oir'yn didn't answer his calls.

He went to the side facing the conjoined cities of J'lem and G'zar and waved. Unsurprisingly, the people of the cities were too busy battling and didn't answer his calls either.

Desperate, Kamal went to the side facing the forest of Amzan and waved. The people-of-the-forest saw him too and, as everyone else, ignored him. They were still angry that Kamal had caused the extinction of their elephants to build his tower. Amzan didn't answer his calls.

What Kamal didn't know is that for many years the poor people of Oir'yn had been stealing ivory from the tower. Its base, formerly solid, was then nearly hollow as if it were made from termite-infested wood. Its structural integrity was compromised. The tower turned so fragile that the feeble vibrations caused by Kamal's waving for help were enough to bring it down.

The collapse of the tower came with a loud blare. People from all land stopped startled to see the column of white smoke rising from where the tower used to stand in the central plain. Many joked about the crazy old man, who was now buried under his rubbish. And after a quick while, everyone went back to their errands without a second thought.

No one ever knew the wonders that were once achieved by the man in the ivory tower.

WITH LOVE, HUMAN

Day 0

We descend from humans. Nowadays, no educated person doubts it anymore. I think that part of the resistance past generations had to accept humans as our distant ancestors is that they looked so different from us. The fossil record reconstruction suggests that they held bizarre near-spherical skulls with flat faces. They likely had furless bodies and walked with a comically-looking bipedal posture. But any physiological or genetic analysis tells that these dissimilarities are superficial. Humans were for sure our evolutive great-grandparents.

Paleontological and geological evidence tells that, like us, humans were cultural beings, driven by innovative strategies, rather than by instincts; fed by agriculture, rather than by hunting and gathering. In their peak, humans counted several billion individuals and lived in large urban concentrations everywhere on Earth of 65 million years ago. Their species flourished in a glimpse of the geological time, for between fifteen and twenty thousand years, and vanished as suddenly as they emerged. They evolved into new beings from which we descent, but not before leaving a clear mark of their civilization into the geological strata. The layer from their era reveals that humans had large industrial capacities as well as imprinted significant environmental impact.

It's always funny to think about the existence of some other intelligent species. We don't know much about the humans, but they built an advanced civilization, in many aspects even beyond ours, as their archeological footprints on the Moon testifies.

The little we know about human culture comes from rare exemplars of pictorial and written recordings, which almost miraculously survived through the ages. Cases were some astonishing conjunction of favorable factors led to the conservation of pieces of material, which should have decomposed eons ago. Archeologists appropriately call them *time capsules*.

One of the most famous of these time capsules is Anne's letters, a collection of epistles' fragments addressed to a female named Anne and written by a male named Mark. Translating them took decades, but it paid off. Anne's letters provided the first glimpse into human psychology and culture. The purpose of Anne's letters seems to be related to some mating ritual. Apparently, if we can take the Letters as representative of human behavioral standards, human reproduction and offspring care were associated with some sort of emotional attachment between mating partners. *Love*, as it was called in human language. It seems to be a kind of emotion that didn't survive in the evolution process that came to us.

It was quite by chance that I became involved with the research of the emotions described in Anne's letters. My college's psychology department was looking for a female student to take part in clinical tests. I enrolled myself out of curiosity. (I've always been fascinated by humans.) I was proud to be selected, although I guess they most probably just flipped a coin.

I'm Alya-daughter-of-Olyar, a student of Natural History; and this is my journal.

Day 1

Today I had my first briefing in the project.

The goal of the researchers—I learned—is to investigate the mating emotions so central in Anne's letters. They believe that although *love* isn't in our repertoire of emotions, our physiology should still be compatible with this emotion. At least that's what tests with lab animals have indicated so far.

Now, the research team wants to go one step ahead and test this hypothesis on someone who could consciously report the feelings. Given the right physical and biochemical stimulus, they expect to be able to activate the primitive layers of our brains where such emotion could reside and make the subject to feel love. Well, the subject, in this case, is me.

I was asked to keep a detailed journal. Here we are.

The research program requires that I get familiarized with Anne's letters. Easy. Then, I'm supposed to go through a chemical-hormonal treatment. That's a bit scarier, but Dr. Michael-son-of-Beckel, the project's principal investigator, granted me all effects would be temporary. They would dissipate within days after stopping the treatment. I'm supposed to be put under environmental stimulus too: resting in a calm place, with soft lights and harmonic sounds on a minor scale. At least this last part sounds pretty inoffensive.

Day 2

Today the chemical and hormonal treatments started. They injected me something and gave me a pack of pills I'm supposed to take during the day. Everyone in the team is very amiable, but they don't tell me anything more technical. I feel like a lab rat. I must go back to the lab tomorrow (and in the next days) to take additional doses of these drugs.

Day 13

I've been under the chemical-hormonal treatment for the last two weeks. And, so far, the only feeling awake is regret. I look hideous. My breasts inflated. My body hair felt. I look like a freaking circus beast. All for science.

Day 14

Today I was brought to a new room in the lab. Different from the white lights from the sterile place I've been under treatment, this room was comfy and warm, decorated with natural materials, and filled with the "harmonic sound on a minor scale" they had mentioned. I was left to rest there for the whole afternoon.

Day 15

In one of the fragments, Mark tells Anne, "You're so much more than beautiful. You're the most amazing woman I have ever met. You're brilliant but kind; tenacious but generous. When I'm near you, I feel complete. When we depart, I feel like a part of my body is missing."

I've read this passage a few times before the experiment even started, and never could really get what Mark meant by such metaphors like "I feel complete" or "part of my body is missing." But reading this same passage now—it's weird—it sounds distinctly significant. It might be placebo talk, but it's like a black and white photo suddenly getting its colors. Difficult to explain, but I think I could empathize with Mark and share the feeling he wanted to deliver.

I'm anxious to tell Dr. Michael about this new experience.

Day 16

I'm supposed to meet Dr. Michael today morning.

I skipped breakfast. I'm not hungry.

I think I'll call sick. I can't meet him looking like this. Looking like a naked ape.

* * *

I met Dr. Michael as expected. The lab sent a car, and a lab assistant convinced me of how important it is to keep a rigid schedule.

I told Dr. Michael about my new feelings regarding Anne's letters. He asked questions, took notes. I expected a bit more from him. I don't know, a little excitement, maybe?

I must continue with the drugs, he told me. And I should keep writing my journal.

I'm not silly. I know that there is something unusual going on with me. Why on Earth do I mind so much about Dr. Michael's opinion on my appearance? In fact, why would I mind about his opinion on anything at all? But I do. And more: I miss him. I miss his presence, his voice. I miss him, "like a part of my body is missing."

Day 17

"Longing for you consumes my days, burns my heart. If I should think of love, I'd think of you. If I should think of love, I'd think of your brown eyes invading my soul without asking for permission. If I should think of love, I'd think of you soft lips smiling while you dream awake, and of how I'd borrow those dreams and make them mine. If I should think of anything, I'd think of kissing you."

Anne, you lucky girl! I may be millions of years too late, but I'm rooting for you, my friend. I hope Mark got that kiss.

As for myself, I'm alone at home. There's no one longing for me. My days are dull, and the only bright moment in my routine is my short meeting with Dr. Michael.

Yes, they wanted to wake up love from its fossil grave. They got it. I felt in love. I'm the first person feeling this emotion since eons. Congratulations to me! Congratulations on this feeling of misery and loneliness. On this feeling that my life is on hold, while the world moves on. On this constant pain in my heart.

When I met Dr. Michael today, I had to constrain myself. At his sight, I wanted to embrace him. Hold him close and feel the warmness of his body. Instead, I sat there in his office, pretending cold neutrality while answering his routine questions. I can't tell whether he knew I was an emotional mess. (Does he know I have a name? "Please, call me Alya," I wanted but didn't dare to ask.)

Shit, what I want from him anyway? To mate and give birth to an offspring? Nope, this is just trivial. We could have done that before any brain experiment. I wanted him here now. Making me company, restoring my peace, calming my heart, kissing my face, turning me whole. And I would be here for him too. Looking at his soul, caring for his dreams, making him happy.

Instead, I just sat there, under the cold white lights of his office, listening to his condescending advice about my diet. At that moment, I truly wanted to jump at his neck and strangle him.

Then, when I walked back home, I stopped in the middle of the campus bridge. I looked down at the parapet. It would have been a long fall, but an easy way out from my pain. Just a morbid thought I erased scared from my mind.

I guess love has a not so caring side, too.

Day 18

[No entry]

Day 19

[No entry]

Day 20

I'm sorry. I couldn't update the journal for a while. More than that, I had no forces to do so. Let me report a brief summary of the disturbing events of the last couple of days.

Two days ago, I returned to the lab, for my treatment, and to meet Dr. Michael. In the sterile room, when the assistant left me alone for a moment, I seized the opportunity to hide with me one of the filled syringes with the drugs I've been administrated.

Later, when I met Dr. Michael alone for our interview, he started the sequence of questions he asked every day. At some point, I stopped answering. I stared at him and told him point-blank, "I love you."

"What do you mean?" he asked clinically, I could say.

"You know what I mean. It means your damn experiment is a success. You woke emotions that had been forever dormant in our brains. But it's much more than that, Dr. Michael. You also open the door into a foreign universe. In this universe, the colors are brighter, and the smells are more intense. The pain is more hurtful, and the pleasure is more glorious. I live in this universe now, and I need you here with me."

I said these words, or admittedly a much less eloquent version of them, and he limited to ask, "What do you want from me?" as if he were reading just another standard question from his lab book.

"You know well enough what I want. I want you to expand the experiment. I want you to take the treatment too. I want you to come into this universe!"

When it was clear that I couldn't convince him, I took the hidden syringe and tried to inject the drug into him!

(What was I thinking? I'm reading these words; I remember my actions. I can't believe either. Madness took over.)

Naturally, my genial plan failed. I hit Dr. Michael's arm with the needle, and, at his scream, a couple of assistants immediately came into the office and immobilized me. As was sedated for the rest of the day.

What was I trying to accomplish? Even if I managed to inject him with the drug, that wouldn't suddenly change his brain chemistry and make him love me back. What did I think I had, a magic love potion?

The single good news is that starting tomorrow, I will begin the detox treatment. This hell is about to end, I hope.

Day 30

The experiment is over. I've made my final report today.

I've out of the meds for ten days now. My mind is getting clear, and the cascade of unfamiliar emotions I underwent in the last weeks starts to be like a memory belonging to someone else. My fur started to grow again.

I'm not quite in my regular mind yet. I still fell Dr. Michael as someone special for me.

Sometimes I wonder whether Dr. Michael wasn't part of the experiment too. It's quite suspicious: during the whole experiment, I was systematically left alone with an alpha male, who would be an obvious target for the induced emotions. Moreover, how likely is that a lab assistant would leave a subject alone to steal drugs at her pleasure? More, how could Dr. Michael's assistants come into his office so promptly when I attacked him with the needle? It was like they were expecting I would do something like that. Maybe paranoia is a side-effect of the drugs wearing off; perhaps the researchers need a good talk with the ethics committee. Well, I have no means to know either way.

This is my last journal entry. I should give all my notes to the research team to be analyzed. I'm still a lab rat. No one has told me anything about the results of the experiment. But I felt that the researchers, Dr. Michael included, were excited. I guess they are going to publish a hot paper. Good for them.

As for me, I'll take a couple of weeks holidays. I need some time for a soul search and make sense of my experience with love. When I come back, I'll work hard to graduate without delay. I want to join a research team and keep investigating humans. I want to study other time capsules like Anne's letters. I think I hold a clear perspective advantage over any other of my colleagues.

I hope one day I'll help understand why humans disappeared and evolved into something else. I wouldn't be surprised if we discovered that it was due to either the paralysis or the madness caused by that nefarious emotion, love.

ABRAM AND SARAI

The Book of Abram

1

"Kill him," the voice whispered in his ears, mixed in the wind. Abram was paralyzed in fear. He was alone at the top of the hill just before the sunset, monitoring the work of the herdsmen. The two words were enough for him to know what was about to come, to him and to his son, Isaac.

Abram was a powerful king. His herd and crops spread in the fields of Beersheba as far as he could see. His chiefdom was protected by more than three hundred soldiers. And Isaac, his only son with his wife Sarai, was his heir.

"Lord Abraham," his servant called, running up the hill towards the tall, muscular patriarch with his wrinkled dark-brown skin and protuberant curly gray beard, dressed in sheepskin and with the head wrapped in a leather scarf. "Excuse me, my lord, we're ready to move the sheep south." Abram woke from his stupor and dismissed the servant with some orders about which borders not to trespass.

Abram took his cane and walked back to his tent where he had his dinner. He ate the lamb stew and the bread without saying a word, which was uncommon for him, who used to lively discuss the deeds of the day during the meal. Sarai, noticing how circumspect he was that night, inquired, "Abram, my dear, is there anything wrong?"

"No. It's nothing," he dismissed. "I'm just worried about how to deal with Abimelech's provocation. He keeps pushing the southern border at the well."

The quarrel with Abimelech had really been in his mind lately. But not that evening. Abram couldn't stop wondering about the windy voice. He hoped he just imagined it. Deep down, however, he knew it was real. The voice had been whispering at him for his whole adult life. And it had been faithful to him. It was more years than he could count since the voice told him that if left Haram, the land of his father Terah, he would be blessed, and his name would be made great. Look at him now, he couldn't have wished better luck. The voice guided him through the drought in Shechem and helped him to make his fortune in Egypt. When he had already lost his hopes of getting Sarai pregnant, the voice told him to be patient. And, in fact, he was blessed with Isaac.

2

That night, Abram slept under the stars near a fire set far away from the tents. He needed to be alone. Abram woke up in the middle of the night when the moon had already set, and darkness reigned. He couldn't see anything beyond the circle illuminated by his fire.

"Kill him," he suddenly heard the whisper. It wasn't an imagined voice. He could listen to it in his ears as if someone were standing just behind his shoulders.

"Kill whom, my Lord?" Abram asked, already knowing the answer.

"Offer me Isaac. Go to the land of Moriah and offer me Isaac."

Horror grew in him as he heard the command. Abram struggled with himself to refuse, but the words didn't form in his mouth. All his efforts were blocked by a knot in his throat, which burst into a guttural scream echoing in the desert. He fell with his face on the earth and wept with indignation. He felt his chest shrinking, like under the weight of a camel. Abram wouldn't dare to voice it aloud, but in his mind, he couldn't avoid questioning why the Lord would make him powerful and wealthy, and ask him to sacrifice the only thing in the whole world he would give up his power and wealth for. Afraid the Lord could hear these unworthy thoughts, Abram recited a prayer as to suffocate them. His tears mixed with the soil, and he didn't mind his face was covered with mud. He rested there and, worn out, slept till the first light of the morning.

3

Abram washed himself at the spring on the way back to the tents. It was early, and he crossed the camp without acknowledging the few women kneading the unleavened bread for the morning meal, who respectfully bowed to him.

At his tent, his called for his servant. He ordered that a small party was prepared to bring him and Isaac for a short peregrination to the land of Moriah, a three days trip. Then, Abram went to see Sarai.

Abram entered his wife's tent, where she was still asleep. "Wake up, Sarai. We need to talk," he called gently. She looked intrigued at him. Abram continued, "The Lord, Hashem, came to me in the fields this night."

"Praise the Lord," she answered with some sleepy automatism. "What does the Lord want from you, Abram?"

"Hear, Sarai, it's not easy what I must tell you," he was searching for the best way to break the news, fully conscious that there were no words that could make it light to any of them. "The Lord commands an offer to Him. The Lord demands Isaac."

Sarai, who was already standing, felt the world turning around her. She gripped at one of the tent's poles to rebalance. "No! Just No!" she cried.

"Listen to me, Sarai. There is no way we can refuse the wish of the Lord. His will is our command."

"Listen, you, to me, Abram. Isaac is my only son; our only son. He will not die because you hear voices in the field."

"Sarai, it's the Lord's voice!"

"How could you tell? For all we know, it could be the voice of the serpent who deceived Eve!"

"I know what I heard, Sarai."

"I don't care. Isaac is my son. He won't be sacrificed! What are you afraid of, Abram? What do you think it will happen if you don't do as the voice demands? That your power will vanish? That your House will fall. That illness will strike us? If so, let it be." Sarai sounded confident and looked sharply at Abram. "Let it be, Abram. I chose those curses over the death of Isaac. And let the curses be multiplied by one thousand, I still choose the misery over our son's sacrifice."

"You don't understand, wife," answered Abram in a condescending but insincere tone, "I'm not afraid of the Lord's curse. I must do it because it's the right thing to do." He was satisfied with his high-ground argument. "We must obey the Lord. We obey Him not for blessing, not to avoid curses. We obey the Lord's commands because we must. That's all."

"I understand well," replied Sarai angrily. "I understand you hear voices, Abram, and I pay the price." Sarai's eyes showed a fury Abram never saw before. She sounded almost guttural, when she added, "You heard voices, and I starved in Shechem. You heard voices, and you had a son with Hagar, before having one with me."

"Shut up, Sarai!"

"You heard voices, and you trade me for the pleasure of the Pharaoh. You heard voices, and you trade me for the pleasure of Abimelech. You heard voices, and you trade me as if I were a whore!"

"Shut up!" Abram's face was sanguineous as if it was to explode.

"Abram, I accepted all the humiliation you imposed on me to this day because I'm your wife, and I must obey you. But you and your voices just trespassed the borders of what is reasonable to ask for from a woman. You will not kill my son!"

"Shut up!" he shouted and hit Sarai in the face, with enough force to throw her across the tent.

Abram left Sarai on the floor sobbing and imploring, "Not my son!"

He crossed the camp determined, calling for his servant, "Prepare the party and prepare Isaac. We depart by the sundown."

4

The sun was red in the west, over the hills of Hatzerim when Abram, Isaac, and two servants, Eliezer and Buz, departed riding donkeys and herding few sheep. Abram looked back and saw Sarai at her tent's entrance. He wished he could go back to atone. He didn't want to depart like that. But she was way out the line. She was his wife and must know her duties to him. Moreover, there was anything he could say at that moment that could make the situation less harsh for them.

During the trip, Abraham was mute. The wise patriarch, who would typically fill the journey with his powerful bass voice, telling stories about how the Lord spared Noah from the flood and so many other stories about all the Houses of Canaan and beyond, was unrecognizable. He claimed he needed to pray. Isaac and the servants respected his wish and traveled in silence as well.

When they camped near Hebron, Isaac took his bow, and with permission from his father, went hunting. It was already dark, and Isaac had still not returned. For a moment, Abram wished he didn't return at all. If Isaac just got lost, Abram couldn't go on with the sacrifice. He would never see his son again, but he would still be alive. Abram was still immersed in these thoughts when he heard Isaac laughing and asking Buz to prepare his prey. Abram walked towards the voices just in time to see Isaac, the brown-skinned handsome boy, handing on the dead hare he hunted. Abram was full of pride. All he wanted was to hug his beloved son. Instead, he went back to the fire and sat quite. Isaac wasn't his anymore. He belonged to Hashem.

The remaining trip occurred without incidents, and the party reached the hills of Moriah in the morning of the third day.

Abram had not heard the voice since his night in the field, before departing. He was cautiously hopeful that the Lord might have changed His wishes. However, at first sight of the hills, he felt the inscrutable presence behind his shoulders.

"Kill him," resounded the dreadful command. "At the top of the next hill, make me an altar, and offer me Isaac."

5

Abram commanded his party to camp at the bottom of the hill. He gave instructions to the servants to wait there and do not interfere while he and Isaac climbed up for their peregrination.

Hushing as to finish the ordeal as fast as possible, Abram started his way up, when he was interrupted by Isaac, "Father, shouldn't we bring a sheep to sacrifice to the Lord?"

"Yes, of course. Bring a ram along, would you?" Abram answered, feeling like a criminal shamefully disguising his demeanor.

"Make me an altar and kill him," the voice insisted.

Abram looked back and saw Isaac following him, herding the ram. He rushed and reached the hilltop much ahead of Isaac. Without putting too much thinking, he started to collect the rocks to build the sacrificial altar, as he had done so many times before. When Isaac finally got to the top, Abram's job was already half-way done. Isaac tied the ram to a bush in a nearby thicket and started to gather wood to help his father. "No, leave the wood there," Abram ordered. "This altar, I must build it myself." Isaac obeyed and rested, observing his father working.

"Kill him," the voice hammered in his ears.

"My Lord, I know my trial well, and I obey. Why do you, my Lord, torture me foisting these hurtful words upon me?" Abram murmured.

"Kill him in my altar."

6

The altar was ready. "Isaac, come here and leave the ram," Abram called. The boy obeyed.

He tried to look Isaac in the eyes, but he couldn't. "My son, you must know, the Lord ... I must ...," he couldn't find words. Abram's face was covered in tears. He embraced a frightened Isaac, who had ever seen his father crying.

Abram gently and easily immobilized Isaac, trapping him with his left arm against his massive body, holding his son's head against his chest. His right arm caught the knife.

Horror crossed Isaac's face, he knew what was about to happen.

"Why, father?" Isaac asked, almost inaudible.

"Kill him. Slay him now, I command!"

7

Not long after Abram and Isaac started the climb for their peregrination, Eliezer came to Buz and wondered, "This is not right. For this whole trip, lord Abraham has not been acting in his normal ways."

"I agree. But what can we do? We have our orders."

"Buz, I fear master Isaac may be in danger—the Lord forbid. Do you think that if anything happens to him, even if inflicted by lord Abraham, we will be welcome back in the camp? If any evil comes towards master Isaac, I'm afraid we will be blamed for it, and even our families will pay for. We must do something, and we must do it now."

These words were enough to convince Buz. Against their orders, both servants started their climb. They got to the top of the hill to witness the abominable scene that would feed their nightmares forever. Abraham had Isaac immobilized against his body and held a knife ready to slice his throat. Abraham's face was distorted into a demonic expression, while Isaac's was frozen in despair. Eliezer and Buz didn't think twice, they ran towards their masters. While Eliezer struggled to take the knife from Abraham, Buz released Isaac and set him at a safe distance, and returned to aid his colleague.

"You're angels of the Lord!" Abraham, already without his knife, shouted hysterical among tears. "The Lord sent you to end my probation! Praise the Lord!"

The servants played along to calm him down, "Yes, we came to finish your probation, my lord. Now, lay down on the floor and rest," said Eliezer. "Hashem will be satisfied by the sacrifice of the ram, my lord." He signaled Buz to bring the ram from the thicket.

Eliezer and Buz slaughtered the animal in the altar, while Abraham watched the ritual obsessively repeating, "Praise the Lord, praise the Lord."

Eliezer approached Isaac, who was still shaking and sobbing, and told him, "Master Isaac, you are a prince, who one day will be my king. You went through an ordeal that only a true prince blessed by the Lord could face. We need you to be strong now, so we can bring you and lord Abraham to the safety of your home. May I count on you, master Isaac?" Isaac assented, cleaning the tears from his face in his arm.

Eliezer and Buz raised Abraham, holding the man by the arms on their shoulders, and carefully dragged him downhill. Isaac followed them. At the bottom of the hill, they cleaned Abraham and his clothes, which were drenched in his urine. They rested there for the night and departed back to Beersheba early in the next morning.

Abraham was catatonic during the whole trip. He was limited to answer to simple commands given by Eliezer, "Drink this water, my lord," "Mount the donkey, my lord." Abraham's dark eyes showed no life, and the strong patriarch, whose imponent figure inspired authority, was reduced to a pitiful shadow of himself when they finally arrived home.

The Book of Sarai

1

Abram left Sarai hurt on the tent's floor. "Not my son!" she implored, sobbing.

Sarai recomposed herself and order her servant to bring her Eliezer immediately.

"Did you call me, lady Sarah?" He politely pretended not to notice the dark bruise around her right eye.

"Yes, Eliezer. How's the preparation for the journey going?"

"Everything is fine, my lady. We should depart by the sundown."

"Good work, Eliezer."

Both rested in silence for a moment.

"Is there anything else, my lady?" the servant asked, knowing that she wouldn't have called him for such a trivial question.

"How's your wife doing, Eliezer? I heard she is with a child."

"She is doing fine, my lady. The child is due on two full moons."

"Congratulations." Sarai looked sharp at him and continued, "May the Lord be with you in this journey, Eliezer. And I pray that my son Isaac will return home in good health. At last, we know that the fortunes of our families run parallel, don't we, Eliezer?"

"Yes, my lady," answered the servant, feeling the full implication of her words.

"You can go now. Please, tell my son I want to see him before the departure."

Eliezer assented and left the tent, knowing that he would have to tread carefully between the wishes of his masters.

Later, Isaac came to see Sarai.

"Did you want to see me, mother?"

"Yes, Isaac. Come here."

He approached her and stopped when he saw her swelling face.

"That's nothing, Isaac," she dismissed. "Come close. Let me hug you, my son."

Sarai hugged Isaac and kissed his forehead. "What's that, mother? I'll be just leaving for a few days."

"I know, Isaac," she tried to hold the tears. "I want you to know that I love you more than anything in this world. I'd give my life for yours without thinking twice. You go now with your father, and I want you to do your prayers." She kissed him again, and he left to continue the preparations.

Sarai remained in her tent for the rest of the afternoon. By the sundown, she listened to the noise of the men preparing to leave. She went to the tent's entrance and watched them from there. Isaac was mounting the donkey, the bow hanging in his shoulder. He looked so much like his father when he was his age. At the time that she and Abram were still only siblings, not spouses.

Abram was already riding his donkey. Instinctively she wanted to wish him good luck, as she always did before he departed. But not this time: his good luck would be her misfortune.

2

The days passed, and Sarai kept the routine, administrating the household, trying not to think on Isaac's ordeal.

In the morning of the sixth day after the men's departure, she was at the spring when a servant came running to tell her the party was spotted, coming back from the north. Sarai ran to the camp entrance, counting the riders at a distance. When she recognized Isaac among them, she prostrated on the floor and gave grace to Hashem.

The men arrived in the camp. Sarai came to Isaac and hugged him. She groped his face and arms as if checking whether he had been hurt. Isaac was in good health, but his distressed look told her he was suffering. In this meanwhile, Eliezer and Buz helped Abram dismount. She approached him, and for a moment, she was startled by his condition. The pale, weak, almost repulsive man hobbling towards her bore no resemblance to her imposing husband.

"Sarai," Abram said, holding her face between his hands, "an angel of the Lord; an angel saved our Isaac, Sarai. We've been blessed." His speech was broken. But these few words were enough to give her a glimpse of what happened in Moriah.

"Bring him inside," she ordered the two servants, pointing to his tent.

After laying Abram on his bed, Eliezer and Buz filled her with the details of the journey and the events at the top of the hill in Moriah.

"You both, you are not to tell any of these things to anyone; not to your wives, not to your neighbors, do you understand me?"

"Yes, lady Sarah," both answered.

"Eliezer, would you stay for a moment?" Buz left them. "Good work, Eliezer. The House of Abraham is forever in your debt. May the Lord bless you and your family."

Sarai was left alone with Abram in the tent. She kneeled down at his side. He was asleep. She touched his forehead and felt he was febrile. She covered him with a skin blanket and let him rest.

Sarai called a servant and sent her to gather all the people at the camp center. She also asked to send her son in.

Isaac came, she took his hands and told him, "Isaac, you've been through a great challenge. And you faced it well. Now, it's time to start anew. Your father loves you as much as I do. And nothing will make him recover sooner than knowing that you also love him. For this reason, I ask you to stay here and take care of your father until his health is restored. Can you do that, my son?"

"Yes, mother."

"There is something else, Isaac. One day you will be the lord of this House. You must know that an honest lord must never lie to his people. However, you must also know that a wise lord must choose carefully how to tell the truth to his people. As a lord, you must remember that there is a difference between how things happened, and what the same things meant. While people can easily gossip about the former, they can hardly grasp the latter. They need their lord to provide them with meaning. You, Isaac, are fated to be an honest and wise lord. And your first lesson on this daring task comes today."

3

Holding Isaac's hand, Sarai exited Abram's tent. The people already waited for her at the camp center, as ordered. She told them, "People from the House of Abraham, I bear wonderful news. The Lord of Adam and Noah spoke to Abraham!"

"Praise the Lord!" someone yelled, "Praise the Lord," others answered.

"The Lord put Abraham through an unbearable challenge. The Lord came to Abraham in the fields and commanded him to sacrifice our only son and heir, Isaac, in the land of Moriah. Abraham, the righteous, obeyed the Lord in every deed to the last consequences. He traveled to Moriah with Isaac and built an altar in the top of a hill chosen by the Lord. Even deeply loving his son, Abraham brought Isaac to the altar, took his knife, and when he was about to sacrifice our son, an angel of the Lord held his hand! Then, the Lord spoke to Abraham again, 'Abraham, do not hurt the boy. You proved your love for the Lord over all things, even over your only son and unique heir. Because of that, I will bless you, and I will make your descendants as numerous as the stars in the sky. As numerous as the sand on the seashore. Abraham, your descendants will take possession of the cities of their enemies, and through your offspring, all nations on earth will be blessed, because you have obeyed me.' And the angel of the Lord took a ram to sacrifice, in place of our son Isaac. These are the news from Abraham and his covenant with the Lord in a hill of Moriah. Now, the lord Abraham rests, as to bear the presence of Hashem wears out even the strongest of the men."

Sarai looked at the people to feel the repercussion of her words. They were in ecstasy. Some yelled praises to the Lord, many others prayed, either kneeling or prostrating. She continued:

"Hashem—the Lord of Adam, Noah, and Abraham—spoke and blessed us. Go now and spread the good news. Go to the neighbor Houses and bring them gifts. As if the Lord has been generous to us, we must be generous to our neighbors. Go and tell the lords of the other Houses that for a fortnight starting in the next full moon, they are invited to be our guests in our lands, and drink from our wine and eat from our bread. As if the Lord has blessed us, we must humbly share this blessing with our neighbors. Praise the Lord!"

THE GRINCH'S TRIAL

"Will the accusation call their next witness?" demanded the judge, from his high tribune.

"Yes, your Honor," answered the prosecutor, a round, old woman, wearing a white makeup over her face, contrasting with her red cheeks. "The accusation calls the defendant, the Grinch, to the bench," she added dramatically, between pointing at the thin, tall figure, covered in green fur, and adjusting her too large attorney's wig, which insisted on slipping from her head.

Murmurs were heard in the galleries, while the defendant took the stand. The Grinch was so tall that, uncomfortably installed at the witness bench, he could look at the judge slightly below him at his right-hand side.

"Mr. Grinch," started the prosecutor, "is it not true that you have obstinately worked to destroy Christmas in several occasions?"

The Grinch sounded genuinely bewildered when he answered, "I worked to destroy Christmas, how so?" His voice was loud and powerful. Curiously, all his phrases started in a deep bass tone and ended in a high pitch, which invariably lent to his slow speech a musical cadence.

The prosecutor was taken by surprise by the Grinch's reaction. She wouldn't expect him to deny the undeniable, common-knowledge fact of his multiples attempts against Christmas. She tried to disguise her astonishment enunciating the events on which she based the accusation. She read them directly from her notes, in a theatrical crescendo, "Are you, Mr. Grinch, going to deny that you maliciously interfered in the Christmas's eve of Melbourne? That you cruelly disturbed the Nativity party of Buenos Aires? That you viciously stole the Noel of Johannesburg?"

"Oh, I see," he interjected with sincerity as if realizing by the first time what the prosecutor meant by her original question. "Mme. Prosecutor, don't you see what all these venues you mentioned have in common?"

"Yes, they have Christmas destroyed by you," she snapped glancing at the jury and bringing laughs to the gallery.

"Silence in the court!" gaveled the judge.

"Clever, very clever, Mme. Prosecutor," the Grinch conceded with a smile, which in his green face looked like a bizarre catenary string hanging from his ears. "What I meant is that all these locations are in the Southern Hemisphere. And all the events you have enunciated took place on the evening of the twenty-fifth day of the twelfth month."

"Are you admitting your criminal demeanors, Mr. Grinch?"

"On the contrary, Mme. Prosecutor. I interfered in each of these parties, but it wasn't a Christmas eve in any of them."

A hiss resounded in the gallery but faded before the judged acted.

"Your defense, Mr. Grinch, is that the evening of the twenty-fifth day of the twelfth month is not the Christmas eve?" the prosecutor interrogated, once more appalled by the peculiar defense line.

"I understand your confusion, Mme. Prosecutor," the Grinch answered condescended. "Would you, please, indulge me and tell which day is today?"

She played along, "Today is the twenty-first day of the sixth month."

"Precisely, today is the longest day of the year."

"And what does this ephemerality has to do with the accusations you are under in this court?" interrupted the judge.

"Your Honor, I don't intend to lecture you on the laws of our firmament, but since my own freedom is under threat by this highly-estimated tribunal of the jury, I'd ask you to give me the liberty to digress. I swear that all will fit in place within a short while."

"I allow it, but be brief," conceded the judge.

"Your Honor, Mme. Prosecutor, you know that the sun makes its wonderful dance in the sky." The Grinch's long arms waved illustrating his words while he explained, "The sun crosses the sky, defining our days. And starting tomorrow, it will set every day a little bit more to the south, than it did in the day before. In this harmonious ballet, the days will shorten until that, on the twenty-second day of the twelfth month, the sun will gift us with its light for the shortest period of a day. Then we will have the longest night. Naturally, through the days following afterward, the sun will reverse its dance, setting every day a little bit more to the north, until we get to the longest day again. This eternal cycle—we call the year—has deep implications for our lives, needless to say."

"Your Honor, I don't see the relevance of this digression," the prosecutor impatiently complained, with the wig covering her eyes.

"I'll be brief now, your Honor," said the Grinch, worried when he noticed one of the members of the jury yawning. "All these ephemeralities are natural to the Northern Hemisphere. Nevertheless, the sun's ballet through the sky draws exactly the opposite pattern in the Southern Hemisphere, where the longest night lies in the sixth month, and the longest day in the twelfth month." The Grinch paused and whispered as if about to tell a weighty secrete, "And now I will reveal to you all here the meaning of Christmas."

The public in the gallery cried, some out of excitement, others out of indignation. The judge gaveled several times before bringing the court into silence. "Please, continue, Mr. Grinch."

"In the Northern Hemisphere, starting at the end of the sixth month, the days get progressively shorter and colder. Darkness and snow. Death and starvation. The depressing weather by the end of the year is only made bearable by the approaching festivities. The Germans, for example, feast on the eleventh day of the eleventh month. The usual lifeless yellow-and-brown palette of their daily dishes gives place to a delicious brown roast goose with violet red-cabbage, beige potato dumplings, green Brussels sprouts, golden baked apples, and russet chestnuts.

"Then, one month later, people get crowded in human-warm Christmas markets drinking hot wine and eating caramelized apples. I personally don't like either of them, but no matter the cold weather, it's always better to stand outside with our friends and neighbors than alone in our heated houses. (Mr. Scrooge, whom I see sitting there in the gallery, had a hard time to understand that simple truth, and he may witness about it.)"

"May the court register that Mr. Scrooge is enlisted as a defense witness!" a high-pitch voice suddenly claimed. Everyone in the court searched for its origin until identifying it belonged to a short, bald man standing behind the attorney's desk, almost hidden by a stack of papers. They realized, somewhat surprised, that the Grinch had a defense lawyer.

"Finally, it comes the so-called 'Christmas eve,'" the Grinch continued. "The family gets together, and people exchange gifts in a millenary tradition going back thousands of years, much before the Christians. Some scholars point its origins to the Roman Saturnalia. They are wrong: this tradition is much, much older, dating back more than nine thousand years when human grandparents first start farming in the temperate zones of Eurasia. I know well, I was there."

Once more, commotion burst in the gallery. Everyone knew the Grinch was old, but no one could guess that he would be so much. Even the judge was amazed by the revelation. "Please continue, Mr. Grinch," demanded the judge, but now playing a higher notch of respect in his voice.

The Grinch concluded, "Thus, in the northern winter, we found the meaning of Christmas: to offer a bit of comfort in the hardest moment of the year." He paused once more to let the idea sink in and continued, "Even if the natural patterns of light and darkness have been disrupted by the electric light bulbs of our clever Mr. Edison, this basic psychology is still embedded in human culture." Thomas Edison, also in the gallery, stood straightening his suit and waved to the court with a seller's smile, distributing his business cards to the people sitting around him.

The Grinch snorted at the scene and proceeded, "Another unrelated Edison, this time my dear friend Annie, once confided to me, 'Christmas is the crazy notion that the longest, coldest, darkest nights can be the warmest and brightest.' I couldn't agree more, and I make mine her wise words." The pretty brunette, sitting in the first row of the gallery, jiggled, barely containing herself, proud with the praise and the buzz of approval in the court.

"For all these reasons, Mme. Prosecutor, I contest that I have ever destroyed the Christmas of Melbourne, Buenos Aires, and Johannesburg!"

The prosecutor, who had been distracted by her own thoughts for a long time already, was suddenly woken up by the Grinch's claim. Goofily adjusting her wig, she rebutted, "On which basis do you contest the accusation, Mr. Grinch?"

"On the basis that there is no Christmas in the Southern Hemisphere in the twelfth month," replied the defendant. "The southern people mindlessly adopted the European traditions and have lived in cognitive dissonance since then. All the myths, metaphors, and allegories we associate to Christmas don't hold in the hot, bright summer days of their twelfth month. They simply don't match the light and darkness cycles that inspired them!"

"Is that a reason to destroy their parties?" the prosecutor questioned.

"I didn't aim at destroying anything. I interfered to help the southern people meet the true meaning of Christmas. I am satisfied, for instance, that in the south of Brazil, we find the equivalent of the Christmas markets in the sixth month—the middle of winter there. People get crowded in St. John's festivities, drinking hot wine and eating caramelized apples!"

"Now, Mr. Grinch, you want to convince this court that you are a role citizen...," pierced the prosecutor ironically with an eye on the jury.

"Look at me, Mme. Prosecutor," he answered, pointing with both hands at himself. "I'm not a role for anyone. However, I have never hated Christmas, as the misconceptions spread by the florid imagination of Dr. Seuss may have led many to believe." The Grinch looked around, searching for the writer, who was in an upper gallery giving his undivided attention to the trial.

"Let me make clear for you and for whoever in this court is willing to listen to me: I love Christmas. I'd do anything to help people love it, too." The Grinch's voice became deeper, filling the courtroom, when he went on, "And for this reason, I despise usurpers, who come late to the party and claim its ownership. Usurpers like that one who brought the charges against me." He pointed at Jesus, who was trying to hide without success in one of the last rows of the gallery. The whole court noisily turned around to gaze at him, with his blue eyes, shampooed long-hairs, and impeccable white tunic.

"Silence!" the gavel resounded.

"I despise profiteers, who sell the Christmas everywhere without caring about its meaning. I despise profiteers, like that one who co-accused me." Now, the Grinch pointed at Santa Claus, who was standing near the door. When the court turned to stare at him, he spat the dark soda he was drinking from a can on his white beard and traditional red clothes, for the delight of the public.

The Grinch rested, and the prosecutor embarrassingly didn't know how to continue with the questioning. She searched her notes while the court waited.

"Mme. Prosecutor, do you have any other question to the defendant?" the judge pressed.

"No, your Honor," she gave up, regretting having called the Grinch to the bench in the first place.

"Mme. Prosecutor, does the accusation still want to proceed with this trial?" the judge inquired, granting her an honorable exit door.

"No, your Honor. We call for immediate dismissal," she answered, clearly relieved.

"In this case, the jury is excused. Mr. Grinch, you are free to go. The court is dismissed!" He gaveled by the last time, for the joy of the gallery.

NOTES ABOUT FUTURE CANVAS

In Future Canvas, I describe human civilization four thousand years from now, living in Dyson caps around the Sun. The story brings some hard numbers, and this note explains how I got them.

The narrator states that "four thousand years since the industrial revolution, and we count one hundred thousand trillion alive souls." It's 10^{17} people, near the carrying capacity of the population (the maximum population size giving the environmental restraints). I got to this figure from a simple estimate of the energy consumption per capita, as follows.

The surface of a spherical cap of radius R with an equatorial opening with width L is

$$S_{cap} = 4\pi R^2 - 2\pi RL.$$

Supposing that all this area is covered by solar panels converting energy with efficiency f_p, the total amount of power available for the caps' civilization is $P_C = f_p P_0 S_{cap}$, where P_0 is the solar power flux at R. Taking $R = 1.5{\times}10^{11}$ m (the distance between the Sun and the caps), $L = 10^{10}$ m (I explain later why), $P_0 = 1361$ kW/m^2 (the solar constant), and $f = 0.8$ (an amount near the thermodynamical limit), we get $P_C = 2.98 \times 10^{29}$ W. The total power available in the caps, P_T, should also include that amount coming from fusion engines, also mentioned in the story. Thus, $P_T = f_F\, P_C$, where f_F is the relative amount of fusion-generated power. If fusion engines contribute at 50% of the converted solar power, $f_F = 1.5$.

To estimate the carrying capacity of the population, K, we should divide the total power available by the power consumption per person, P_p:

$$K = P_T / P_p.$$

To get P_p, consider that the current global power consumption P_{CC} is about 5.76×10^{26} W for a population (p_0) of 7.5 billion people. Supposing that in the caps this consumption is larger by a factor f_i, we have $P_P = f_i\, P_{CC} / p_0$. If, $f_i = 100$, the power consumption per person in the caps is 7.68×10^{12} W. With this value, the carrying capacity of the caps' population is $K = 5.8 \times 10^{16}$, about the 10^{17} people mentioned in the story.

Such population size can be reached within a few thousand years. The logistic equation for population growth tells that the population as a function of time is given by

$$p(t) = K / (1 + A e^{-rt}),$$

where $A = (K - p_0)/p_0$ and r is the relative growth rate coefficient. Supposing that r remains constant at the current value, 1.1% per year, the population would reach 10^{16} people within about 1500 years from now.

I mentioned that the equatorial opening in the cap is $L = 10^{10}$ m. One of the functions of this opening is not to shadow the outer planets. Among these planets, Mars is the one whose orbit deviates the most from the solar system invariable plane, $a_{Mars} = 1.7°$. This value sets the cap opening at $L > 2R\sin(a_{Mars})$, about $L = 10^{10}$ m.

The story narrator also mentions their city is "a cylindric craft with about two-kilometer radius and half-kilometer long, where 1.5 million people live in one hundred concentric stores." We can estimate the population density from these numbers. Supposing that each store has a height h, the habitable surface of the city is

$$S_{city} = 2\pi H_{city} \sum_i (R_{city} - ih),$$

where the sum runs from $i = 1$ to $N_{stores} = 100$. With $H_{city} = 0.5$ km, $R_{city} = 1$ km, and $h = 5$ m, we get $S_{city} = 234$ km². For 2.5 million people, this surface renders a population density of 10645/km², about the same as in current Paris or Manhattan.

ACKNOWLEDGMENTS

I've written many of the stories from this collection over the last five years. Although this is the first time they appear in a book, several of them were published in an old blog I kept, "Much Bigger Outside." I would like to thank the people who followed the blog and gave me feedback and support to keep writing. Among them, Kakali Sen, Rachel Crespo-Otero, Shuming Bai, Dilmas Souza, Marcos André Borges, and my recently deceased father, Paulo C. Barbatti.

I'm also in debt to Anderson Tomaz, Marcelo Percia, Fabris Kossoski, Oliver Weingart, Sylvicley Figueira, Adriano Martins, and Paulo Marcio Barbatti. Through many discussions (and obscene amounts of beer), they helped me polish my thoughts.

I live in a strange nomadic world. All these people are loving friends from different eras, spread over many countries, and most of them don't even know each other. I care about each of them dearly, and I fantasize that my writing creates a world where they all share the same table.

I've been ruminating some of the ideas I developed in this book for a long, long time. The first versions of "The end and the life" and "The borderless truth" were written two decades ago. However, no matter it's an old story or a recently written one, I'm deeply grateful for the support in many levels from my friend, partner, and wife, Carla Barbatti, in our long journey together through the world.

Fontaine, August 20, 2019.

MB

ABOUT THE AUTHOR

Cosmopolitan defines Mario Barbatti. Don't let the Italian-sounding name deceives you. Born and bred in Brazil, in the last sixteen years, he and his wife, Carla, have lived and worked in Austria, Netherlands, Germany, and France, as well as visited three dozen countries.

Mario Barbatti is a renowned scientist. He earned a Ph.D. in physics in 2001, and since 2015, he is a professor of theoretical chemistry in the University of Aix Marseille in France. He has published over 150 papers in prestigious scientific journals, which have been cited over four thousand timed by his peers. In 2019, Mario Barbatti was awarded an ERC Advanced Grant, the most prestigious and competitive research funding in the European Union.

"One Billion Faces" is Barbatti's first incursion in the fictional realm. The stories composing this book span a wild variety of topics and styles, to contemplate our role in the universe, often from an unexpected entanglement of fantastic realism and hard science fiction.

To know more about the author, visit www.barbatti.org. You can also meet him on Twitter (@MarioBarbatti) or on Facebook (www.facebook.com/mario.barbatti).

ONE BILLION FACES

BY MARIO BARBATTI

García Márquez and Arthur C. Clarke meet for coffee. "One Billion Faces" brings to life the unexpected entanglement of fantastic realism and hard science fiction.

In a collection of seven short and ten flash stories, the renowned scientist and 2019-awardee of the ERC Advanced Grant Mario Barbatti invited us to contemplate the extremes of the human condition. Either delving into the psychology of some of the founding myths of the western culture or speculating about our place in the universe on unthinkable time scales, "One Billion Faces" is a profound imagination journey.

The amazements and frights of the near future, the superation of all human limits within thousands of years, the wonders of our descendants down millions of years from now, the reemergence of life after all stars are burnt, these are some of the themes carefully crafted into the absorbing stories of this book.